ID MG

D0409759

'I used to daydream about this,' she said. 'Sitting in the car beside you— the wind blowing through my hair.'

He turned towards her and smiled. 'Well, you were the only girl I ever imagined beside me in the red convertible. Although I did wonder if the colour would clash with your hair.'

'Is that why you bought a blue car?' Meg teased, feeling more at ease with Sam than she had since his surprise return.

'Maybe it was,' he told her, but he wasn't smiling now. He was looking at the road ahead and frowning—just slightly. He couldn't possibly have bought a blue car because it would go better with the hair of someone he hadn't seen for thirteen years, Sam told himself. No, not even subconsciously.

But the thought had rattled him—the way just about everything to do with Meg was rattling him.

Meredith Webber says of herself, 'Some ten years ago, I read an article which suggested that Mills & Boon® were looking for new medical authors. I had one of those "I can do that" moments, and gave it a try. What began as a challenge has become an obsession, though I do temper the "butt on seat" career of writing with dirty but healthy outdoor pursuits, fossicking through the Australian Outback in search of gold or opals. Having had some success in all of these endeavours, I now consider I've found the perfect lifestyle.'

Recent titles by the same author:

THE DOCTOR'S MARRIAGE WISH
  Crocodile Creek: 24-Hour Rescue
SHEIKH SURGEON
COMING HOME FOR CHRISTMAS
THE ITALIAN SURGEON*
THE HEART SURGEON'S PROPOSAL*
THE CHILDREN'S HEART SURGEON*

Jimmie's Children's Unit

BRIDE AT BAY HOSPITAL

BY
MEREDITH WEBBER

MILLS & BOON®

All the characters in this book have no existence outside
the imagination of the author, and have no relation
whatsoever to anyone bearing the same name or names.
They are not even distantly inspired by any individual
known or unknown to the author, and all the incidents
are pure invention.

All Rights Reserved including the right of reproduction
in whole or in part in any form. This edition is published
by arrangement with Harlequin Enterprises II B.V.
The text of this publication or any part thereof may
not be reproduced or transmitted in any form or by
any means, electronic or mechanical, including
photocopying, recording, storage in an information
retrieval system, or otherwise, without the written
permission of the publisher.

MILLS & BOON and MILLS & BOON with the
Rose Device are registered trademarks of the publisher.

Webber, Meredith

Bride at Bay
Hospital / by
Meredith Webber
                LP

1743165

First published in Great Britain 2006
Large Print edition 2007
Harlequin Mills & Boon Limited,
Eton House, 18-24 Paradise Road,
Richmond, Surrey TW9 1SR

© Meredith Webber 2006

ISBN-13: 978 0 263 19533 0
ISBN-10:   0 263 19533 0

Set in Times Roman 16½ on 20 pt.
17-0207-49672

Printed and bound in Great Britain
by Antony Rowe Ltd, Chippenham, Wiltshire

BRIDE AT
BAY HOSPITAL

CHAPTER ONE

MEG heard the voice as she grabbed an armful of clothes from the built-in wardrobe in the main bedroom.

Her bedroom!

Or it had been until today.

Or officially yesterday.

'Vacant possession!' The voice was deep, and powerful enough to carry right through the old wooden house without being raised to shouting level. 'I stipulated vacant possession.'

Whoever was on the receiving end of the cold statement must have had a quieter voice, for Meg heard nothing of the explanation. But by then she was scurrying through the kitchen, intending to slip out the back way, down the steps and across to the cottage next door without being seen.

'He'd have had his bloody vacant possession

if it weren't for the flu,' she muttered to herself, as exhaustion from an extra night shift weakened her bones and sapped her confidence so self-pity lurked perilously close.

She didn't do self-pity!

'Not that he's arrived with a furniture van all ready to move in,' she told her cat, who'd come out of the cottage to see if any of the clothes were trailing a belt or ribbon that would make a good plaything.

Meg dumped her load on her bed and crossed to the window in time to see the realtor's car drive off.

Great! She could nick back over and get the rest of her stuff. One drawer full of undies— that was it!

She'd give him vacant possession!

But as she walked through the kitchen a sense of loss overwhelmed her, and she faltered as she remembered the happy times she'd had in the old house. Up until now, she'd only considered the financial aspect of moving—her father had let her have the house at a nominal rent because he'd understood her dream.

But now...

No, she wouldn't think about her father—or about the dream.

The dream her mother said was foolish…

Anger swamped her maudlin mood. Anger at her mother for deciding to sell their old holiday house—anger at the stranger who had bought her memories. Muttering dire threats she would never carry out, she stomped back into the bedroom.

The stranger, tall and dark, face shadowed by the window behind him, was twirling one of her G-strings round his fingers so the little red hearts on it made a circle of red against the white—red, white, red, white.

'Put that down!' She gave equal emphasis to each word, her own red anger, barely controlled, whirling in her head.

'Megan?'

The stranger looked from the panties to her, back to the panties, and then frowned before he said her name again—this time with even more incredulity.

'Megan?'

She snatched the garment from him and turned away, certain it couldn't be Sam—knowing from the rapid pulsing of her heart it had to be.

'Megan.'

Not a question this time but a statement, accompanied by a touch of his hand on her shoulder. A mist of rage and something that could almost have been hatred filled her head, and she didn't need the pressure of that hand to make her turn.

'What is this, Sam? Some variation on the return of the prodigal son? Some revenge thing that you had to buy my house? Turn me out? Well, great! Have the bloody house! Have your vacant possession! And you can have my knickers, too, because I'd be damned if I'd wear them after you've touched them!'

And with that she stormed away, head held high but cheeks aflame with heat, while her heart skittered about in her chest like a terrified rabbit in search of the deepest, darkest burrow it could find.

'Well, that went well.'

Sam sighed as he looked at the minute undergarment she'd dropped on the floor in her hurry to get away. Then he shook his head.

What was Megan doing in the Bay? And how

could he have known she'd been living in the house? He'd bought it from the trustees of her father's estate and had been told the house was tenanted, but never in his wildest dreams had he considered Megan might have been the tenant.

Megan…

Something in his chest scrunched tight as his head repeated her name, but he had it on good authority from any number of women that he didn't have a heart, so it had to have been some other organ scrunching.

Or perhaps a muscle.

Intercostal muscles tightening his ribcage because of a perfectly natural trepidation about this return to the town of his childhood.

That would explain the scrunch.

He crossed the empty room and looked out at the wide sweep of blue water, wondering why the hell he'd come back, then, feeling the pull of the beauty in front of him, he realised just how dangerous this return might prove. That he, to whom emotional control was so important, should feel that pull was surely a danger signal.

That he should feel something at the sight of Meg was doubly dangerous.

Meg…

She'd stormed out through the kitchen. Where had she been going? He hadn't seen a car outside, and she hadn't brought in a suitcase to collect her last few items of clothing.

He followed the route she'd taken and looked out the back door, across to the cottage where he'd grown up. He'd had a note from the realtor recently. Something about a new tenant, good references, six months' lease, and did he object to a cat…?

A cat!

He hadn't objected to the cat, but now he saw it, a sealpoint Siamese, sitting erect and alert at the back door, he knew for sure Meg was the tenant. Right through her childhood there'd been such a cat—a cat which had been both friend and confidant to the shy, gangly, red-headed kid she'd been.

How could fate have been so unkind to Meg that he and she were now transposed in their residences? No wonder she was upset. But why, if she was living in this house, had it been sold?

And why, if she'd wanted to keep it, hadn't she made some arrangement to buy it?

He hardened his heart against the softness caused by thinking of unkind fates and Meg in the same sentence. He reminded himself they were virtual strangers now and, though neighbours once again, need have nothing more to do with each other apart from a neighbourly nod from time to time.

'And this, Dr Agostini, is our director of nursing, Megan Anstey.'

It was just after nine the following morning, and Sam was following Bill Roberts, the hospital administrator, through the building, knowing he'd need a week or so to get all the names straight in his head.

Except for this name.

'You're a nurse?'

'You're a doctor?'

OK, he'd sounded startled, but he'd done nothing to deserve the huff of derision that had accompanied Meg's question.

'You two know each other?'

'Good guess, Bill, though not, I hasten to add, in the biblical sense!' Meg said, her vivid green eyes challenging and defying Sam as she added, 'You'll find most of the local staff—female staff in particular—know Dr Agostini. Just wait till the word gets round that Sam's back in town. Flu recovery rates will pick up immediately.'

'Is that what you call a warm friendly Bay greeting?'

Sam's voice was silky smooth—dangerously smooth—and poor harmless Bill was obviously wishing the floor would open up and swallow him.

'We've already done the greeting bit,' Meg replied. 'And now, if we've finished chatting, I'm down twelve staff and am needed on the wards.'

She whisked away without waiting for a reply, her heart thundering in her chest, her hands shaking, her knees so wobbly it was a wonder they were holding her up.

Sam next door was one thing. She was usually too busy to see much of her neighbours. But Sam right here, in *her* hospital?

'Have you heard? Sam Agostini's back in town—not only back in town but acting super for the hospital. I always assumed he'd be in jail by now.'

Coralie Stephens was both ward sister and the main trunk of the hospital grapevine, so this conversation shouldn't have surprised Meg, but hearing Sam's name on Coralie's lips made her feel sick. Even sicker than the news he wasn't passing through.

Coralie West she'd been back then, new in town, and the first conquest Sam had flaunted in front of Meg that terrible Christmas.

But at least Meg now had an explanation for Sam's presence—acting super. Apparently the new medical superintendent they'd been expecting had been delayed. Though why, if he was only acting, would Sam have bought a house here?

She fended off all the unanswerable questions competing for attention in her head and concentrated on the staff roster on Coralie's desk. Coralie was busy filling in her ward secretary on the legend that was Sam Agostini—the bad boy of the Bay.

'Gorgeous, he was just gorgeous—darkly handsome with the most arresting blue-green eyes. But wild! You wouldn't believe the things he'd do. The story is he once swam across the bay for a bet and you know what the sharks are like out there, and he certainly put one of his mates in hospital after a fight. I was there that night. Boy, could he fight.' She paused. 'I wonder if Wade knows he's back in town.'

Meg heard the smugness in Coralie's voice, and felt sorry for Wade Stephens. The man deserved better than his wife trying to rekindle an old affair with Sam Agostini!

'We're still in dire straits with staff—can you do an extra shift?' she asked the sister, hoping to bring the conversation back to work-related matters.

Coralie's reply was swift.

'No way! Not today. I've a hair appointment.'

Coralie? Whose hair looked as if she cut it with a knife and fork?

Hair appointment?

Meg forbore from comment, but inwardly she was cursing Sam's arrival back in town. As if the hospital wasn't in enough trouble, with the epidemic of summer flu, without women who should know better going dippy over a good-looking scoundrel.

Maybe he had a wife.

Surely he'd have a wife!

She hadn't noticed a wedding ring…

But, then, she'd barely noticed anything about the man—except that it had been Sam.

'There are no sharks in the bay—it's too shallow,' she told the ward secretary, who was new in town. 'The sharks just made for a better a story.'

The young woman smiled at her, but the avid way she turned her attention back to Coralie told Meg just how disruptive Sam's return might be.

'And this is the medical ward.'

Bill's voice alerted her to the fact that the guided tour of his precious hospital had caught up with her, but as Coralie rushed forward to welcome Sam, enveloping him in a hug, Meg moved away. She couldn't avoid giving him a wry smile as she passed him to remind him of their shared revulsion of all things soppy and sentimental when they had been inseparable holiday playmates as kids.

Sam fended off Coralie West, or whatever she was called now, as best he could, offering what he hoped was a disarming but suitably neutral smile.

'Great to see you,' he said, while in his head he

wondered about his sanity. Bringing his mother back here had been one thing—but after she'd—

He cut off the thought, concentrating instead on the information Bill was giving him. Complex medical cases were transferred to Brisbane, but good visiting specialists meant they could handle most things.

'And our consultant surgeons are terrific,' Bill continued, leading him towards the surgical ward. 'Top class.'

Were they following some hospital round routine that meant Megan was in front of him at every turn? She was bending over the desk, her hair, a darker, richer red than it had been when she'd been young, falling forward so it cast a shadow on her rather stern profile, her tall, lean figure curved towards the girl behind the computer, her long, slim legs bare of stockings and as white as Meg's skin always was.

As kids they'd stretch out on the beach and she'd rest her leg against his so they could marvel at the contrast of her whiteness against his tanned brown skin.

'Put more sunscreen on!' he'd order, and she'd

mimic his order to annoy him, but obey, knowing just how burnt she'd get if she didn't cover up all the time.

'It goes red then blisters, then peels and we're back to white!' she'd complained. 'Red, white, red, white!' And for some reason he thought of the tiny panties he'd swung on his finger the previous afternoon.

Meg in a sexy thong?

In his experience women only wore such things for a man.

'So we can do it.'

He had no idea what Bill had been talking about, and at some stage, while he'd been lost in his memories, Meg had whisked away again.

Bill was called to the phone so Sam continued on his own, wandering into what was obviously the children's ward. Meg again! Sitting on the edge of a bed, talking to a young lad who had his left leg and right arm hooked up in traction.

Sam paused by the desk.

'That's Brad Crosby,' a nurse who introduced herself as Sue explained to him. 'Broke both legs and one arm trying to fly off the veranda of his house. He's always in trouble, that boy. Single p—'

'Sue!'

Meg's voice made them both turn, whatever Sue was about to say cut off.

'Is the physio due to see Brad today?'

Sue checked on her computer as Meg came across to the desk, while Sam moved across to talk to the boy.

'Flying, huh?' he said as he drew closer. 'What did you use for wings?'

'Garbage bags,' Brad said with a sigh. 'The packet said they were extra-tough but they ripped right through the moment they took my weight. Not at the Velcro where I'd stuck them on my clothes but the plastic itself tore.'

'Tough luck, eh?' Sam said. 'Guess you have to rethink the whole idea.'

'No way!' Brad told him. 'My mum'd kill me if I did it again. Besides, Meg said to wait until I was a bit older when I get a bit heavier then I can try kite surfing. You know, on a small board at the edge of the water when a strong wind is blowing. Meg says it's just like flying.'

'Meg told you all this?' Sam turned towards the woman in question, who was now bent over Sue's shoulder looking at the computer screen.

'Meg's cool,' Brad replied, a hint of hero-worship in his voice. 'And she doesn't nag. Not that Mum nags much, and when she does it's only 'cos she worries about me—that's something else Meg told me.'

Sam sat with the boy a little longer, learning more of the original uses to which Brad had put his apparently endless supply of Velcro, but when Meg left the ward he said farewell to his new young friend and followed her, catching up with her near an alcove that housed a public phone.

'Did you cut Sue off to spare my feelings?' he asked, looking down into a face that was both familiar yet extraordinarily new to him.

'Cut Sue off?'

The slight flush in her cheeks told him she was prevaricating.

'When she was about to make a remark about Brad being the product of a single-parent family,' Sam persisted.

'I cut her off because I don't like the staff making

judgements about patients, and they all know it.'
Defiant emerald eyes met his. 'I hate the way a
label can be slapped on someone and judgement
made because of that label. As if people are
nothing more than varieties of tomato sauce.'

Sam felt a smile twitching at his lips. This was
definitely a Meg he knew, standing up for the
rights of others—ready to take on the world if
necessary. That hadn't changed!

'And Brad's brand of tomato sauce had "single
parent family" on the label?'

Meg grinned at him.

'Same as yours—Bad Boy Brand!' she said,
but the words slipped in one ear and out the
other, his mind too occupied with the jolt he'd
felt inside his chest when Meg's face had lit up
with that cheeky smile.

'I don't know how to be with you.' The words
blurted from his lips, and a frown chased Meg's
smile away.

'How to be with me?'

Sam knew the smile he offered was a foolish
one, and shrugged his confusion away.

'That came out wrong, but this is so weird,

Megan. I feel I know you yet I don't know you. The old Meg—well, we usually picked up right where we left off…'

Wrong analogy. Right where they'd left off last time had been a disaster—a hurtful, painful, unmitigated disaster.

Was Meg remembering?

'It's been thirteen years, Sam,' she reminded him, revealing nothing beneath an ultra cool and controlled exterior and a polite smile he knew was false. 'We've both changed.'

'Have we?'

He shouldn't be persisting with this conversation but couldn't stop himself.

'Of course we have. We were kids thirteen years ago—now we're adults.'

'Are we?' He caught himself just in time. 'Dumb question! Of course we are, although do you really feel different—feel like an adult—all the time?'

Meg's cool façade cracked and she smiled again, enthusiasm bubbling back to the surface with the memories.

'Right now I feel fifteen again—or thirteen—or eleven—having one of those earnest, interminable discussions we used to have. About evolution or religion or morality or—'

'Friendship,' Sam reminded her, taken back himself. 'Would you lie for a friend? Die for a friend?'

'No to both—wasn't that always my stand? That there had to be another way around the problem?'

'Oh, Meg, there you are.' A nurse Sam hadn't met came hurrying towards them. 'Ben Richards is on his way in by ambulance—heart pains. Jenny phoned, asked if you could meet him.'

'Ben Richards? The Ben Richards I—'

'Put in hospital,' Meg finished for him, but she said it softly so the nurse, who was walking away from them, didn't hear her.

'Damn!' she continued as she hurried down the corridor, Sam following in her wake. 'His father died from heart disease and Jenny's been warning him this would happen. Ben's overweight and he drinks too much.'

'Then *he* hasn't changed,' Sam muttered, uncertain how to tackle this new challenge in the 'returning home' scenario.

'He's a patient and whatever that was all

about—it was a long time ago,' Meg reminded him, although she'd have given her eye teeth and probably a couple of front ones as well to know what *had* happened.

'I *should* be able to manage, Sister Anstey,' Sam told her, coolly polite, the nostalgic moments of accord between them lost again. The Sam who could always hide his feelings was back in control again. 'In fact, if I remember rightly, you're the one more likely to lose your temper in pressure situations.'

'I didn't put Ben Richards into hospital with concussion and a broken jaw thirteen years ago,' Meg snapped, then regretted the jibe when she saw the pain on Sam's face.

It was the one time he'd lost control! No one had ever found out what had started the fight but, whatever it was, the memory still had the power to hurt Sam deeply.

And seeing Sam in pain still affected her…

Oh, dear!

She led the way towards the emergency room doors where the ambulance bearers were already unloading their patient.

'ECG's OK but we can only do a rhythm strip so it's hard to tell. He was in a lot of pain. We gave him aspirin and 5 milligrams of morphine IV, notes all here.'

Meg took the initial assessment forms, signed for them, then handed back one copy to the ambulance bearer before turning to introduce Sam.

'Cal Johnson, meet Sam Agostini, acting medical super at the hospital.'

'Sam Agostini? That really you, Sam? Didn't end up in jail after all!'

Ben's voice was hoarse as he interrupted the introduction, but he obviously wasn't upset at meeting his old adversary. He grabbed at Sam's hand and held it in both of his.

'I hope you're a good doctor, mate. My Jenny couldn't cope with something happening to me right now.'

Sam leaned forward to reassure him as tears began to stream down Ben's cheeks.

'Our baby is sick.' The big man's voice was hoarse with emotion, his face twisted with grief. 'So little and so sick—leukaemia. Did you know boys with Down's syndrome are prone to it?

Hardly fair, is it? And just when Jenny needs me to be strong, and supportive for her and the kids—for little Benjie—look at me. Useless bastard that I am!'

'We'll have you out of here in no time and, knowing this town, there'll be someone out there with Jenny right now, helping with the kids.' Sam rested his other hand on Ben's shoulder. 'But first things first. Let's see if we can find out what's causing your pain and what we can do to stop it happening again.'

He glanced up at Meg.

'Get him straight onto a twelve-lead ECG. I'll take blood for testing. Does the hospital have its own path lab?'

'We can do basic stuff. In Ben's case cardiac enzymes, white-cell count, ESR, U and E, glucose, lipids and a clotting screen.'

Sam frowned at her.

'Are you sure you're not a doctor in disguise?'

Simple enough question, one would have thought, but once again he watched as Meg's face lost colour. Anguished green eyes were raised to his—anguished green eyes that caused pain in the part of his chest where he didn't have a heart.

'Quite sure,' she said quietly, walking beside the trolley as Ben was wheeled into the trauma room.

She was all efficiency —this woman he hadn't expected to see and certainly hadn't expected to feel anything for. Working with swift, sure movements, she changed Ben's oxygen feed from the bottle on the ambulance trolley to the hospital supply, attached the leads to Ben's chest, added more leads for a heart monitor then moved the monitor screen so Sam could see it.

And as she worked she talked to Ben—nothing kind of talk, explaining what she was doing, teasing him gently in a way, Sam realised, that boosted Ben's spirits far more readily than sympathy would have done.

She passed Sam a catheter to insert into Ben's arm, first to take blood for testing, then so drugs could be administered into his veins. Her fingers accidentally brushed his when the exchange took place, and she glanced up at him, bewilderment showing on her face, as if whatever she had felt puzzled her.

What he'd felt puzzled him as well…

'It's bad? Is that what you think?'

Ben's anxious query told Sam he must be frowning.

'No way, mate!' he assured the man. 'In fact, the exact opposite. There are no visible signs from the ECG that your heart's playing up.'

'But the pain!' Ben protested. 'It was like an elephant sat on my chest.'

'I've heard it described more elegantly,' Meg told him.

'And I've heard it described exactly like that,' Sam put in. 'The pain is definitely a symptom that something's not right, which is why we've got you hooked up to monitors that are telling us how your heart and lungs are working, and the level of oxygen in your blood. We'll know more when we get the results of the blood tests back from the lab.'

He glanced enquiringly at Meg who assured him the blood had been sent.

'What can happen,' Sam continued, 'is that the arteries that feed your heart muscle become clogged with plaque, and if they're not getting enough blood to the heart and the heart muscle isn't getting enough oxygen from the blood, you'll feel pain. I'm giving you nitroglycerin to open up those blood vessels so more blood gets through, and the monitors will tell us how the drug is working. We'll let you rest for a while but eventually you'll be having a whole battery of tests. Have you been referred to a cardiologist before this?'

Ben shook his head, then grinned at Sam.

'Only been in hospital once before,' he said, 'and you know why that was!'

Sam stopped still, an image flashed before him. *A big group of them had been in the street outside the cinema complex, having celebrated the last day of the school year at the movies. He'd been thinking about Meg, who had been due to arrive the following day, when one of the girls—had it been Coralie West?—had come up and slipped her arm through his, suggesting they nip away for a kiss and cuddle at the beach.*

He'd backed off, trying to find a way to say no without hurting her feelings, then suddenly Ben, who'd probably been sneaking rum into his Coke, had raised his voice.

Made an unbelievable accusation…

Sam's head and fist had exploded simultaneously, sending the much taller Ben flying backwards. A mate had grabbed Sam, but he'd shaken him off, while Ben had clambered back to his feet and surged towards his adversary. Ben had been tough, farm-hardened and cunning in his choice of punches, but in the end, it had been rage that had won the fight for Sam.

Although it hadn't been a win—it had been a loss.

A loss of innocence…

Of joy…

Of love…

CHAPTER TWO

'First lot of test results, Doctor.'

Something in the nurse's voice made Sam look more closely at her.

'I should know you, shouldn't I?' he said and the pert blonde smiled.

'Thirteen years is a long time, Sam,' she said. 'I'm Kelly Warren, Eddie's younger sister.'

'The pest!' Sam remembered, grinning at the woman. 'You look great. How's Eddie?'

'He's still in town. He took over Dad's pharmacy. Boy, did he miss you when you left.'

Sam nodded. Eddie had been a good friend— Sam's one true friend, apart from Meg—yet he'd never bothered to keep in touch. But that was how his friendships had been—surface things— because he'd never been good at letting people get too close—letting people in.

Except for Meg…

He smiled at Kelly.

'I'll be sure to look him up,' he promised her, taking the test results and studying them, nodding to himself as he walked back into Ben's cubicle.

Meg was holding Ben's hand and talking quietly to him.

Comforting him, Sam told himself, though he couldn't have said why he needed to find an excuse for Meg's presence.

Or the hand-holding.

Get over it!

'OK!' he said, edging near enough to the bed for Meg to have to move. 'Your blood has an increase in something we call CPK. That's a cardiac enzyme—creatine phosphokinase, if you want the whole story. An increase in CPK usually indicates a heart attack even when the monitors don't show it, and the level of CPK indicates how severe or otherwise the attack was. You've been lucky, Ben. It was very mild. Next we'll do an echocardiogram to see if we can see any damage to the heart muscle and there'll be further tests once you see a cardiologist.'

'We have a visiting cardiologist who comes twice a week—Tuesday and Thursday,' Meg offered. 'He'll be in town tomorrow and we can make arrangements for him to see Ben here.'

'Here? I can't stay here,' Ben protested, trying to sit up. 'I've got to get home to Jenny and the kids. Benjie's due for more chemo tomorrow.' He broke down again, tears pooling in his eyes as he added, 'We both come in with him every time.'

Sam felt Ben's anguish but before he could explain why he couldn't be released, Meg was talking.

'Benjie's tough,' she reminded their patient. 'He'll be OK just with Jenny, although, as he has it right here in the hospital, if you're OK, there's no reason why you can't be with them. But right now the best thing you can do for Jenny and all your family is to rest and get better.'

Sam nodded, adding, 'And you've no option but to stay here. We're giving you drugs to keep your arteries open and to dissolve any clots that might be lurking in them. We need you on the monitors so we can see how the drugs are working.'

And to make sure you don't have another heart

attack. As he left the cubicle, Sam couldn't help thinking of the number of times he'd seen a second more severe heart attack occur in patients while they'd been in A and E. Chest pain caused anxiety, anxiety caused blood pressure and heart rate to increase, and the higher the blood pressure and heart rate, the harder the heart had to work. Unfortunately, a heart already battling to work properly didn't take kindly to an extra workload.

'Are you going to move him to a ward?'

Meg joined him outside the curtains, seeing his worry for Ben in Sam's narrowed eyes and furrowed forehead.

Sam hesitated for a moment before shaking his head.

'If the hospital had a coronary care unit I would, but right now the best monitoring he can get is right there, for a few hours at least. We'll move him later. His wife's coming in?'

'As soon as her mother gets out to the farm to mind the kids.'

'How many kids do they have?' Sam asked, concern warming his voice, surprising Meg because he'd always remained detached from other people's problems. Except for hers… 'I know about Benjie! Talk about rotten luck—the little fellow getting leukaemia. I guess the only good part is you're able to give him chemo here so there's less disruption to the family.'

'Not without a fight,' Meg told him. 'The powers that be insisted at first he go to Brisbane, but Ben's a farmer—he can't get away for any length of time, and there are three older girls as well, so it wasn't exactly easy for Jenny to go either.'

Sam's smile twined around Meg's heart.

'You did the fighting?'

'The whole town fought,' she told him, not wanting him to think her special—more especially not wanting smiles that affected her heart. 'The mayor wrote directly to the premier, every doctor in town wrote to the Health Department, and ordinary, everyday citizens bullied their local MPs until an agreement was reached. The Bay hasn't changed much in that everyone pulls together in a crisis, and Benjie's leukaemia is just one of many uniting forces I've seen since I came to live here permanently.'

'Why did you come back, Meg?'

It was the last question she'd expected and she hesitated, uncertain how to answer. She couldn't lie to save herself, her tendency to go fiery red a dead give-away. In the end she settled on part truth.

'Cheap accommodation.'

It was a flippant reply and Sam obviously read the warning she'd hoped to convey.

'None of my business, huh?' he said, then he changed the subject. 'Ben's wife—Jenny, is it? Do I know her?'

Meg heard a hint of apprehension in his voice and frowned at him.

'Are you surprised people remember you?'

'I've been gone thirteen years, Meg. Of course I'm surprised.'

'Then you didn't think through this "back to the Bay" decision too well. Why wouldn't people remember you? You were into every-thing—the swimming champ, the football captain. Jenny was Jenny Wilson—her parents still have the bakery in town. Mrs Wilson used to give us finger buns whenever we went in there. Mind you, she probably gave finger buns to every kid in town.'

'Of course. Jenny Wilson was in my year at school.' Sam spoke slowly, as if he was only just beginning to consider the implications of his return to the Bay. And for a moment Meg almost felt sorry for him.

'Exactly,' she said, quelling the feeling before it had time to take hold. Then curiosity got the better of her. She asked the same question he'd asked earlier. 'Why *did* you come back?'

Sam's face closed. Someone else, standing in front of him, might not have noticed the wiping of all expression from a face that didn't give away much in the first place. But Meg had seen it happen before—often enough to recognise that whatever minor truce might have existed between them for a few minutes was now over.

Not that she should be worried about it—Sam Agostini was none of her business.

Though not yet late—just after seven—it was dark by the time Sam drove back up to the Point and along the road to his house.

His house?

In his mind it was still the Anstey house.

He glanced towards cottage but there were no lights on. No doubt Meg was still performing one of her seemingly limitless roles at the hospital. Family counselling it had been when he'd called in to check on Ben Richards late that afternoon and had found Meg there with Jenny and various other family members who all remembered him—and registered their surprise he wasn't in jail—but were strangers as far as he was concerned.

He parked his car and walked up the front steps—hoping the removal men had successfully completed the unpacking for him. I don't care what goes where, he'd told them, sure they'd be better able to place furniture and stack cupboards than he would be.

He wondered what they'd made of the drawer full of feminine underwear in the main bedroom.

On the front veranda, he stopped and turned towards the view, seeing the sweep of the bay and far out a faint twinkle of light from the island. A fisherman on the beach? Someone camping in the sand dunes?

His chest began to ache again and a savage

anger swept over him as he realised Meg had been right.

He *hadn't* thought through his return to the Bay.

Oh, he'd considered all the practical aspects of it—the business side of things, the opportunities it presented—the reasons he'd had to come. But if he'd considered any emotional impact, it had merely been to remind himself he was older now—a mature adult—and in spite of what an interfering, psychiatrist ex-girlfriend had once said about him carrying emotional baggage, he'd been totally convinced that all the past was right where it belonged—safely in the past.

A movement down on the beach caught his eye, and though the moon had not yet risen, there was enough light reflecting off the water for him to see it was a woman. A woman with a longish stick in her hand—writing in the sand.

He moved without thought, back down the steps, across the road, easily finding the grassy track that led downwards through the tall gum trees to the park, across it to the beach.

But once there he hesitated. Megan—and he'd known with an inner certainty it was her—had moved on so she was almost at the point. If he waited just a minute, she'd be out of sight.

As would he be of her…

He paused in the shadows until he could no longer see her then walked towards the water, which splashed with tiny, sloshing waves against the gritty sand. The tide must be going out, for the words she'd written hadn't been washed away.

Megan Anstey, in beautiful curly cursive script. Meg's hair might have darkened to a rich auburn, and her gangly figure filled out with woman-hood, but her writing hadn't changed.

He followed the big letters to the end and found that after them she'd written 'Megan Scott'.

Megan Scott?

Sam frowned at the surname.

'Megan Anstey', written on the beach, used to be followed by 'Megan Agostini'.

But that had been thirteen years ago!

Didn't stop him frowning.

Was Megan married to this Scott, or just in love with him?

Engaged?

He didn't need to know.

It was none of his business.

So why was he still following the writing?

'Megan Anstey' again.

Without knowing why, Sam felt immeasurably better, though the next name jolted him.

Not so much a name as the word 'Megan' then a question mark. Was there someone in Meg's life she was thinking of marrying?

Why wouldn't there be? She was young, attractive, vibrant, sexy—

Sexy?

Had he ever considered that word and Meg in the same breath?

'Reading other people's mail?'

He looked up to see her barely ten feet away, the sand having dulled any sound of her return.

'Sand writing's like postcards—fair game,' he reminded her, staring at her shadowed figure and wondering if perhaps his ex-girlfriend had been right and he did have an excessively large load of baggage from the past.

He certainly felt as if he was carrying something heavy right now. Heavy enough to make his chest feel tight and his muscles bunch with tension.

'Were you looking for me?'

For the last thirteen years, a voice inside his head responded, but he knew this wasn't true. He'd thought of Meg from time to time, but—

'No. I just wandered down for a breath of fresh air before going into the house to see what kind of a fist of unpacking the removal men have made. I paid for the whole job—packing and unpacking.'

This is a ridiculous conversation, his inner voice mocked, but Sam was surprised he'd managed an almost rational reply.

'Money no object, then?' Meg asked, in a voice he didn't recognise as her's. Meg had never been snide or catty but, then, that Meg had been a girl. Thirteen years was plenty of time to find a bit of snide and catty!

'It was more a matter of time. I wasn't due to start up here for another month, then I had an SOS from an old friend who was coming up as the medical super at the hospital. She couldn't leave Brisbane and, knowing I was heading this way, asked if I'd step in for her.'

It was still a ridiculous conversation to be

having with Meg, but at least it was keeping his mind away from thoughts of Meg the girl.

And the sand writing.

From Megan Question Mark?

Almost keeping his thoughts away...

'You were coming anyway? When Bill said acting super I thought maybe you'd bought the house as a holiday home and were just here for however long you were acting.'

Meg knew she must sound strained, but she'd come to the beach in an attempt to regain her inner peace and composure—to try to get rid of all the turbulent emotions that seeing Sam—and knowing she'd be seeing more of him—had stirred inside her. Now, just when it had seemed to be working, here he was!

She studied him. Tall and strong-looking. He'd naturally enough filled out over the intervening years so his broad shoulders looked well muscled and his body solid—manly!

'You were coming anyway?' she said again, thinking she'd be better getting her mind off the subject of Sam's body.

'I was coming anyway,' he echoed, but there

was such sadness in the words Meg stepped towards him, responding to some inexplicable need within her—or within him.

'Sam?' she murmured, and he leaned towards her.

The waves whispered softly on the sand, the early stars shed soft silver light about them, and Sam's head bent towards hers, slowly, slowly, as if willed by something beyond his control—something that went against his wishes and judgement and common sense.

A barely heard 'Meg...'

The kiss was soft at first—tentative, testing—and the taste of Sam was both new and yet familiar. Too new and too familiar for Meg not to respond—tentatively testing for herself. It was a kiss that both sought and gave her comfort, though comfort was far from the other reactions it was generating.

Need, desire, heat—all the reactions Sam's kisses had generated in the adolescent Megan long ago—not diminished by time, but heightened and strengthened by the maturity of her body and the very obvious maturity of his.

Or was it his skill as a kisser that was changing her response? Skill and mastery that seemed to be drawing the very soul from her body and sweeping away any will to resist.

This was the kiss of her dreams but with a real Sam, not a fantasy, yet fantasy was there as well and she was sixteen again, kissing the teenage Sam who was soon to become her lover...

'Meg,' he repeated softly, and though his voice seemed to be coming from a far distant planet, enough of her name reached her to make her draw away.

As she moved, the spell was broken. She stared at him in disbelief—disbelief levelled at herself, not him.

Then very deliberately she wiped her hand across her lips and said, 'Don't you ever do that to me again!'

Would he remember? she wondered as, with tears puddling in her eyes and agony tugging at her heart, she walked away from him.

'Megan, wait! Meg, I can explain!'

His voice followed her, but she wasn't going to stop. Wasn't going to risk being caught in that web of sensuality he wove so effortlessly around her—not again.

Would he remember his own gesture—his own words—from all those years ago?

She doubted it, and somehow that thought made her blink back the tears and straighten her shoulders as she crossed the park, determined not to show Sam Agostini her pain.

Sam watched her go, remembering back to when he'd given Meg good reason to write 'Megan Agostini' in the sand.

Meg at sixteen, arriving for the Christmas holidays thirteen years ago, flying from her house to the cottage, in through the side door and into his bedroom, casting herself into his arms and kissing him full on the mouth.

Over the previous three holidays—Easter, June and September—their relationship had changed. Somewhere along the line Meg had grown breasts and put a little padding around her hips so they swelled gently out below her tiny waist. While looking at her legs, he'd seen not their paleness but their sexy length. Hormones and libido had done the rest and two childhood best friends had become not lovers but girlfriend and boyfriend, together exploring their developing sexuality. The sheer delight of moonlight walks on the beach and stolen kisses had been all they'd wanted from each other during the shorter holidays, although by October they were sure enough of how they felt to discuss taking their relationship further.

How innocent we were! Sam thought, grimacing at the memories.

Christmas holidays, they'd decided, would be the perfect time for both of them to lose their virginity. They'd have seven weeks together—or as together as they could be. Seven weeks! It would be like a honeymoon—only before marriage, not after it.

But when the day had come, when she'd come bursting into his room, flung her arms around his neck and kissed him, he'd wiped her kiss off his lips, told her never to do it again, and broken her heart.

Lost his own at the same time, Sam suspected, for he'd felt nothing for the pain he'd caused his mother over those particular holidays or for the girls he'd kissed and left without a second thought, or for the trail of chaos he'd blazed through the Bay until Meg's father had stepped in, offering to pay his tuition at a private school in Sydney for his final year at school—finding his mother a job down there so they could be together.

Now, when it was too late to say thank you because Meg's father was dead, he understood Dr Anstey had done what he had out of kindness, but back then, poisoned by words Ben Richards probably didn't remember saying, it had served to prove to Sam that Ben's jibe was true.

He *had* to explain…

He caught up with her as, breathless from her rush up the steep path, she rested a moment, leaning against the big eucalypt at the top of the track.

'Meg! I thought you were my sister!'

Were the words breathless because he'd run to catch her, or because of their ridiculous nature?

Meg spun to face him.

'You thought I was your sister?' An echo of utter disbelief. 'How could I possibly have been your sister?'

The answer, though slow coming, was

obvious. Her disbelief deepened but with it came uncertainty.

And then pain.

'You thought my father— *My* father?'

And now the demon doubt arrived, cutting into her so deeply she had to bend to ease the pain. Was that why her mother had been so anxious to sell the holiday house after her father's death?

It was all too much for Meg.

'How *could* you think that? How *could* you?' she yelled, swiping the stick she still carried towards Sam, catching him across the cheek, before turning and racing towards the cottage.

Sam wanted to follow—to explain he no longer thought it—but that wasn't the point and he knew it. Meg had adored her father, and he her. They'd shared the same hair colouring, quick temper, utter loyalty and soft heart. The careless words—Sam's urgent need to explain the past— had made things worse, not better.

Though wasn't he always making things worse?

Wasn't that his forte in relationships?

Wreaking havoc in the lives of the women he courted, leaving a trail of destruction in his path?

He muttered angrily to himself as he made his way home.

Home! That was a laugh! How could the Anstey house ever be his home—with Meg living in the cottage next door, a constant reminder of how things had once been?

He changed his mind and went back down the track to the beach. Maybe a run would make him feel better. And maybe the huge full moon, rising in orange-gold glory above the waters of the bay, was made of cheese!

He should have followed her—explained it better. He'd have to try again.

Have to hope she'd understand.

Now, why would he hope that? he wondered as he pounded along the beach.

Because one kiss had told him so. One kiss had proved that the fire he'd found lacking in every relationship he'd ever had since that momentous day was still there between himself and Meg.

He sighed again and turned to run back, accidentally obliterating the question mark after 'Megan' as he did so.

Accidentally?

He climbed back up the steep slope for the second time that evening, feeling slightly better for the exercise.

Then he saw the ambulance outside Meg's cottage and his heart didn't need exercise to accelerate.

Pulse pounding, he ran towards it, then felt foolish as he saw her emerge from the cottage in the fluorescent-taped garments of a paramedic.

'Don't tell me you're an ambo in your spare time,' he said, hoping she'd not hear the anger he was feeling—anger born of relief that she was OK.

She gave him a frigid glare and he knew she was considering not answering him at all, but she could hardly keep up a 'not speaking' effort when they had to work together.

'SES paramedic,' she said briefly. 'State Emergency Service.'

She was climbing into the ambulance as she spoke.

'What's happened?'

She frowned before answering.

'It's practice night. Phil picked me up in the ambulance because tonight we're explaining to some new volunteers exactly what equipment an ambulance carries and how we use it all.'

'I'll come, too. I'll follow you in my car—that way I can give you a lift home.'

Was he out of his head? She was barely speaking to him and here he was offering her a lift home?

He had to explain…

'Phil will give me a lift home.' *And you can go to hell!* The words rang unspoken in the air between them.

'Do I know Phil?'

Sam knew, even before Meg made an exasperated noise, that it was a stupid question, but his head was demanding to know if Phil might be the admirer she'd been thinking about on the beach.

Not, of course, that it was any of his business.

Meg had made that more than clear, even before he'd delivered his killer blow!

But just so there could be absolutely no mistake in his mind, she replied, 'No, Phil's new to town. So chances are you never knew his sisters either!'

Ouch!

Feeling foolish, and angry, and frustrated that

he couldn't immediately explain what he'd said earlier, Sam peered at the bewildered Phil. He was relieved to find the young man was barely old enough to shave, then felt even angrier with himself that he was pleased.

But it was stubbornness more than anger that forced him to add, 'I'll still come. A local doctor should know about the working of the SES.'

'Perhaps another time,' Meg said coolly. 'Because that's not my pager beeping, and Phil doesn't have one, so I assume it's yours.'

Foolish didn't come into it! She'd annihilated him. He walked swiftly back to his house, phoned the hospital in response to the page—Benjie Richards had been admitted with breathing difficulties—and Ben was insisting he be discharged.

He arrived at the hospital to find Ben stripping off his monitor leads.

'Just how do you think Jenny will cope if you have a second attack?' Sam said to him, and the big man slumped back on the bed.

'I can't just lie here like a lump of useless meat while Benjie might be dying in another room.'

'Benjie's not dying,' Sam said firmly, although he hadn't yet met the little boy or received a report on his progress. 'Jenny's with him and she'll come back and report to you as soon as she knows he's settled down. And I'll go and see him and report back to you as well.'

Ben's anxiety lessened.

'Would you really?'

He sounded pathetic but Sam knew the greatest concern with heart patients was the level of stress they felt.

'Of course I will, you chump. Right after I've checked your drip and reattached those leads. Chances are Benjie's been given something to sedate him and he'll be asleep by the time I get there, so you might see Jenny back here before you see me.'

Sam settled his patient back in bed, and made sure he was as comfortable as possible with all the leads running from his body.

'Sedation works,' Ben told him. 'Benjie's got a bit of asthma but he gets upset when he gets an attack.' He gave Sam a slightly shame faced grin. 'Guess I could do with a bit as well,' he said, then added in a more serious voice, 'But not just yet, Sam. I need to know the boy's all right.'

Sam heard the love in Ben's voice and felt a momentary pang of jealousy. For all the suffering he might have been through, Ben still had a loving wife and four children to hold to his heart.

He, Sam, had nothing.

Not even a heart, he sometimes suspected.

He shook his head. He'd been so upbeat about coming back to the Bay so why the maudlin mood swings?

'Sam! Oh, Sam, it's good to have you back.'

Jenny cast herself into Sam's arms and gave him a huge hug as he walked into the children's ward.

'When Ben told me, I could hardly believe it!' She'd stepped back and now she looked up into his face. 'So you made it through medical school—you became a doctor! It's what you always wanted to do, isn't it?'

Sam grinned at her.

'You're the first person who's remembered that ambition. Everyone else I've seen has wondered that I'm still out of jail.'

'That's only because you went crazy that last

summer, Sam. But I knew you for a lot longer than one summer holiday.'

'And believed in me,' Sam said softly.

Jenny smiled and tucked her arm through his, leading him towards a cot where her little boy lay sleeping, an oxygen mask strapped across his pale face.

'First Ben, now this little fellow,' Sam said gently, and Jenny squeezed his arm.

'We'll cope,' she told him. 'We've got good at coping—the Richards family.'

'Good on you,' Sam said, easing away so he could bend over the cot and look at the tiny child.

In spite of the slight malformation in the facial features caused by the errant gene in Benjie's make-up, Sam smiled to see the resemblance of the little boy to his dad.

'He's Ben all over again,' he said to Jenny, reaching out to tuck the little starfish hand beneath the sheet.

'Spitting image,' Jenny agreed. 'Everyone talks about it.'

'And the leukaemia?' Sam asked gently.

Jenny drew in a deep breath.

'We're fighting it, Sam. That's all we can do. Benjie's a fighter, too. Although I know the chemo is so much easier to take now, it still knocks him around for a day or two, but then he bounces back and is his normal, boisterous self. Although today—'

'It might just have been the asthma attack.' Sam was quick to assure her, although he was wondering whether Benjie had seen his father collapse with pain—seen the ambulance—and, little though he was, understood some of the significance of it.

'I hope so,' Jenny said, bending to kiss her son, then turning to Brad, who was the only child still awake in the ward. 'I'm leaving you in charge,' she told him. 'You ring for someone if he wakes.'

Her instruction made Sam turn towards the desk, wondering if perhaps the hospital was so short-staffed a patient had to keep watch. But the nurse at the desk just smiled at him, leaving Jenny to explain as she accompanied him back to Ben's room.

'Brad's been in and out of hospital so often he thinks he owns the place,' she said. 'So it's natural to kid him around.'

She paused, then added, 'And he loves Benjie, so he *will* watch over him.'

'It sounds to me as if everyone loves Benjie,' Sam said, and saw Jenny's smile bring a glow to her cheeks.

'Oh, they do,' she whispered, then she went ahead, entering Ben's room, eager to tell him his little son had settled down to sleep.

CHAPTER THREE

SAM sat in his office for a while, pretending to read the information in the files on his desk, but his mind wasn't taking in much, wondering instead what time Meg might get home—and whether it would still be early enough for him to explain.

In the end he gave up and wandered back to the children's ward where Jenny was sitting talking to Brad while keeping a watchful eye on her sleeping child.

'Could I see Benjie's file?' he asked the nurse, who lifted a bulky package off the desk.

'All of it or just the recent admissions?' she asked.

He looked at the full file and realised he wouldn't have time to read it all tonight. Maybe Jenny could explain.

She'd kissed Brad goodnight and was back by Benjie's bed.

'Ben's fretting and I really need to be with him, but I hate leaving Benjie.'

'He's sleeping soundly, so I would think keeping Ben's anxiety levels down would be the main concern,' Sam said, resting his arm on her shoulder as she watched her sleeping child.

'Come on,' he said, turning her with a slight pressure of his hand. 'As we walk back you can tell me about Benjie. How old is he and where's he up to with his treatment?'

'Don't they call that diversion therapy?' Jenny said, smiling at him as they walked into the corridor. 'He's two, diagnosed three and a half months ago. Dr Chan, the paediatrician here in the Bay, picked it up straight away and we did go to Brisbane for the initial intensive treatment, then for his catheter to be put in and for the five day block of treatment in the second month. What we're up to now—the fourth month—is one daily 6-mercaptopurine tablet, weekly tablets of… Is it methotrexate?'

Sam nodded, remembering the protocols from his stint in paediatrics as an intern.

'He comes in for monthly injections—I forget what that drug is—and later in the month we do five days of steroids. While he's at the hospital for that day—tomorrow, it's supposed to be—they do more blood tests and the results of those tests will determine if the tablets need to be changed.'

'The dosage altered,' Sam confirmed, as they paused outside Ben's room to finish the conversation.

The curtains had been drawn across the internal windows so it wasn't until they entered the room that he noticed Meg sitting by Ben's bed. Again!

Sam watched as she stood up and kissed Jenny on the cheek. Watched as she carefully avoided either looking at him or acknowledging him.

'I wondered if you wanted me to stay with Benjie tonight so you can be with Ben,' she said, and Jenny's smile and warm hug provided all the answer anyone needed. 'I was filling Ben in on the SES meeting while I waited for you. He agrees we need a new captain but old Ned's been there so long, no one has the heart to tell him it's time to leave.'

The conversation continued for a few minutes, giving Sam the opportunity to watch the two women. They were obviously close friends— because Benjie was hospitalised so often?

'Jenny was great to me that Christmas,' Meg said, as he followed her out of the room a little later.

He knew immediately what Christmas she meant, but what bothered him was Meg's seeming ability to read his mind. Or was she simply making conversation to get past the tension between them?

Not such a bad idea.

'You don't have staff to cover the little boy on a one-on-one basis?' he asked. The awkwardness between them had increased since he'd mentioned the sister thing. It was like a glass wall—solid and impenetrable—but talking medical matters made pretence at normality easier.

'Not unless the child is desperately ill. I've spoken to Kristianne, the doctor on duty, who, with Dr Chan, his paediatrician, admitted Benjie, and he's OK, though I don't know what the on-cologist will say tomorrow.'

'You have an oncologist come in just for him?'

Meg's smile made him realise how incredulous he must have sounded. It also managed to pene-trate the glass wall and cause quivers in his chest.

'We have one on-line—a direct link so we can talk to him and he can talk to us. Kristianne took more blood from Benjie when he came in, and we'll flick those test results through to the oncologist as soon as they're available. It'll be up to him whether Benjie has treatment tomorrow or not.'

It all sounded quite sensible to Meg, so why was Sam frowning at her? Was he thinking about that ridiculous statement he'd made earlier?

'You went to an SES meeting,' he said, accu-sation biting into the words. 'So how come you know all this? Who admitted him—taking blood, all the details?'

'I rode back to the hospital with Bill, who's also in the SES. I guessed your page meant some kind of crisis and I don't like to have stuff hap-pening that I don't know about.'

Sam smiled at her.

'You never did,' he reminded her, and though she knew she shouldn't be feeling anything for Sam, she found herself smiling back.

They stood by Benjie's bed, looking down at the sleeping child. Meg leant forward to adjust the blue striped beanie the little boy wore.

'Local football colours, aren't they?' Sam asked, feeling strange that he and Meg should be standing beside a small child's cot.

Strange, yet somehow right...

And he didn't do emotion?

'Bay Dolphins,' she confirmed. 'They've adopted Benjie as a mascot. They donated all the gate takings from their final game towards the Benjie Fund that helps out with the expenses of the family.'

'Did they win?'

Meg turned and smiled, then thrust her arm in the air as she said in a loud whisper, 'You bet they did. Go, Dolphins!'

'For someone who only ever spent holidays in the Bay, you've become a local from the look of things,' Sam said.

But it was Brad who answered.

'That's because she cares about stuff apart from just patients in a bed,' the child informed him.

'Do you?' Sam asked directly, turning his clear-eyed gaze from Brad to Meg.

'Of course I do, but so does everyone else in the profession. Most of the people in your profession, too, I would have thought.'

'Not entirely,' Sam argued, pleased that, with the help of two children, they'd managed to find their way back through the glass wall, to some kind of neutral territory. 'I'm not saying specialists don't care about the whole person, but they do tend to become quite focussed on their main interest. Look at orthopods who only operate on hands.'

'But they're doing their best to achieve a positive outcome for the patient, not just his hand.'

'Maybe,' Sam said so dubiously that Meg laughed.

'There always was a touch of the cynic in you,' she told him. 'Now, can you help me move this chair?'

She pointed towards a big reclining lounge chair.

'To over here by Benjie?' Sam asked.

'No, that I could manage myself. I want to take it through to Ben's room for Jenny. There's another one near Brad I can use.'

'Don't the other wards have facilities for family staying over?'

Meg studied him.

'Do you really want an answer or was that just a conversational question?'

'Why wouldn't I want an answer?' Sam had moved towards the chair and was now manoeuvring it towards the door.

'Because you're acting super—not here permanently. Most people passing through wouldn't care.'

He frowned at her.

'Well, I do, OK?'

Taking up a position on the other side of the chair brought her closer to Sam—this new caring Sam—closer than she liked, so it was good to have something to explain.

'Because serious cases are transferred on to larger hospitals we rarely have patients ill enough to warrant family staying with them. But I believe parents should be able to stay with their sick kids so recently Bill found the funds to buy these chairs.'

Blue-green eyes met hers across the chair as they pushed it through the door, and she saw the faint mark on his face where her stick had struck him.

He'd thought she was his sister?

Disbelief was yelling the question in her head, but if Sam could behave as if he hadn't delivered that deadly blow only hours earlier, so could she.

'Working on getting them for the other wards, are you?' he was asking, and though his lips weren't smiling she could see a teasing gleam in his eyes. A teasing gleam that melted her bones and made her heart do little tap dances in her chest.

Oh, no, not again! You cannot fall for Sam again!

But is it again—or still…?

'It wouldn't be a bad idea,' she said, stiffly formal as she tried to hide the effect he had on her. 'But money's always tight.'

Together they managed to get the chair to Ben's room and when Jenny began to question Sam about Ben's heart attack, Meg slipped away.

He's not here for ever, she reminded herself. You can handle it.

But could she?

She went through to the children's ward and shifted another big chair, this time close to Benjie's cot. The little boy was still sleeping peacefully, and would probably stay that way throughout the night. They had a monitor on the mattress, the device usually used for babies with suspected sudden infant death syndrome. It had an alarm that would sound if Benjie stopped breathing. But for Jenny and Ben's peace of mind, Meg would stay by his side.

She drew a fingertip along his arm, marvelling at the super-smooth skin.

'Keep fighting, Benjie,' she whispered to the little boy, then she sank down into the chair beside him.

Exhaustion, both physical and emotional, flooded through her as she let her body relax in the soft recliner. The physical she could explain. She'd been doing double shifts for a week now.

The emotional exhaustion was also explainable but far less easy to set aside. If she felt this way after Sam's first day in the hospital, how was she going to feel after a week—or a month—or however long he intended working here?

But it wasn't so much Sam's presence causing emotional havoc as the sister thing. Why hadn't she stayed when he'd told her? Listened to him explain?

Because she'd been too shocked to think straight!

How could such an impossible, inconceivable, horribly revolting idea have got into his stupid head?

She thought back—way back—but even after thirteen years the memories were still vivid. They had spoken on the phone the previous weekend—silly, excited, soon-we'll-really-be-together talk—lovers' talk. So what had happened in the intervening week?

She didn't know of any major events earlier in that week, but the night before she'd arrived, cool, controlled Sam, who rarely showed any emotion at all, had had a fight.

He'd put Ben Richards in hospital with a broken jaw. The first move in seven weeks of madness and mayhem when he'd torn through town like a tornado, barely escaping being locked up for drunken behaviour, losing his licence for a multitude of offences, not least of which had been speeding down the Esplanade, and, most hurtful of all to Meg, dating every teenage female in the caravan park.

Meg pushed the hurtful memories aside, turned in the chair and snuggled down against the cool leather, closing her eyes but unable to close her mind to the memories that swarmed like bees inside her head.

Was she asleep?

Sam stood in the doorway of the children's ward and looked at Meg, curled sideways in the big recliner, her dark red hair falling across her face.

He wanted to explain the remark he'd made earlier—the statement that had sent her flying across the road to the sanctuary of the cottage. But she was obviously exhausted, and this was hardly the time or the place for explanations.

So what should he do?

Walk away?

He swore viciously to himself, cursing his insensitivity in blurting it out that way, cursing her for not listening earlier—on the beach—when he'd wanted to explain and could have done it rationally.

Then he looked at the bent head and his anger dissolved into nothingness.

This was *Meg*. How could he *not* know how best to treat her?

Because the Meg he'd known had been sixteen—a girl. This was a woman—and, to all intents and purposes, a stranger.

Her eyes opened as he stood there. Had his thoughts woken her?

He walked into the room, nodding at the nurse who sat in the glow of a nightlamp at the desk.

Meg straightened in the chair and spoke quietly to the nurse.

'Why don't you take a break?' she suggested. 'With me here, and Dr Agostini prowling around the wards, it's a good opportunity for you to grab a coffee and something to eat.'

The young woman stood up immediately, thanking Meg and slipping out the door so swiftly Sam wondered if the tension between himself and Meg was so strong it could be felt by others in their vicinity.

He came further into the room, checking the beds where the children—even Brad—lay sleeping, then he reached the chair where Meg still sat, and squatted down beside it.

The hazy look in her eyes told him she'd been sleeping.

'Sam?'

And having slept, had she forgotten her animosity towards him so his name came out so sweetly from her lips?

But memory returned all too swiftly—the soft lips thinning and the look in her eyes suddenly wary.

Then anxious.

'Is Ben all right? He hasn't had another attack, has he?'

'Ben's fine,' he told her.

'Then—?'

Her eyes took in his position—still squatting beside her chair—silently asking the question she hadn't finished.

And though he hadn't wanted, or expected,

this reunion with his old friend, Sam's heart—it *had* to be his heart—ached that things should be so awkward between them.

'What I said earlier—I need to explain.'

Her eyes narrowed as she sat up in the chair and folded her arms defensively across her chest.

'Haven't you done enough explaining for one night?'

He touched her arm and felt her reaction as nerves and muscles stiffened.

'You know I haven't.'

'Well, maybe I've done listening,' she told him. 'I'm so deep in disbelief that you could think such a thing of my father—let alone of your mother— it'd take a mountain of explanations to get past it.'

'Your father paid my school fees for the next year.'

Sam's words killed the bees buzzing in Meg's head, blotting out everything but the deadly implication they held. She shivered under the weight of it, and Sam reached out and grasped her shoulder.

She certainly didn't have the strength to move away from his touch, or to object when he gently eased her back against the softness of the chair.

'What was I supposed to think, Meg?' Sam demanded, taking both her hands in his, though why she was allowing it she didn't know.

Perhaps because her thoughts were so out of control right now she needed something— anything—to anchor her to reality.

'I've gone about this all the wrong way, Meg,' he was saying. 'But we need to clear the air between us. It started the night before—the night before you came. We'd been to the movies, a whole gang of us—and Ben had been drinking.'

'Ben Richards?' A name she knew—another anchor.

Sam nodded, and she saw the dark head bend towards her in a silly parody of an on-bended-knee proposal.

'Ben made a stupid remark about…' He hesitated, looking up into her face, his blue-green eyes pleading with her but asking her what? To listen?

Or to understand?

She'd listen—she doubted she had the strength to do otherwise.

Understanding wasn't something she could promise.

'He said something stupid to the effect that I shouldn't kiss any of the girls in the Bay because any one of them might be my sister.'

The gruff voice, the anguished eyes told Meg how Sam had felt more vividly than words could have managed.

'He made out...'

He couldn't go on, getting up and moving away, his back turned as if even after thirteen years the pain was so great he couldn't let her see it.

'Made out your mother was...' Meg whispered, unable to finish the sentence as her own throat was choked with emotion.

'A whore, slut, whatever you want to call it!' Sam finished for her, speaking softly so the children weren't disturbed, back in control though she could see the effort it cost him in the set of his jaw and the tension in his shoulders.

'No wonder you hit him,' Meg muttered, unable to believe the pain Sam must have felt. Then common sense reminded her it had been a long time ago, and she tried to consider the subject more rationally.

'But you knew your mother wasn't like that,' she protested, and saw Sam's eyebrows rise.

'Did I?' He gave a helpless shrug. 'I knew her as a mother, not as a teenager going out with boys. *You* know, because we talked about it often enough, that she flatly refused to tell me who my father was. Said she had her reasons. Then Ben drops his poison, not missing your dad in the list of candidates for my paternity, and your father turns around and pays my school fees at a private school. What was I supposed to think, Megan? What was I *supposed* to think?'

Meg shook her head.

'Of my *mother*?'

Anguish bit into his words, hurting Meg almost more than she'd been hurt thirteen years ago.

Of course her father paying his school fees would have confirmed all Sam's worst imaginings. Her own heart was racing at the idea that it could have been true, although she knew there must be more—that Sam must have finally found out some truth—because his kiss on the beach had been anything but brotherly.

She tried to think—tried to get her brain

working—knowing there was something big she was missing here.

'But your mother would have said something —said we shouldn't see each other—if it *had* been my dad,' she pointed out, and Sam turned, his face pale.

'Unless she hadn't known!' he ground out, holding out his hands as if in supplication. 'Can you imagine the hurt I did my mother when I accused her of that? When I refused to believe her when she assured me I could kiss any girl in the Bay without fear of incest? I hurt her, Meg, and kept on hurting her. Oh, we reached a kind of truce when we shifted down to Sydney, but I always knew she was pining for the Bay and selfishly believed it was a punishment she had to bear because she was so obdurate about not telling me.'

'But her not telling you must simply have confirmed your worst fears,' Meg whispered. 'Confirmed your impression that she didn't know!'

'Exactly!' He nodded, pacing restlessly around her chair and Benjie's cot.

Meg stared at him, sure there should be something she could say to ease the pain his memories were causing. But it was late, and she was exhausted—physically and now emotion-ally—and her head was filled with cotton wool.

He saved himself, turning back towards her, the past wiped off his face—all expression wiped away. He'd always been good at hiding his feelings...

Too good!

'You're exhausted. I shouldn't have brought all this up tonight of all nights but having started...'

'I'm glad you told me,' Meg managed, although she wasn't sure it was the truth.

He nodded, bent to look at Benjie, rested the backs of his fingers lightly against the child's cheek.

Meg could feel his pain and longed to comfort him but, not knowing how, could only reach out and touch him lightly on the back. But this was Sam—the old Sam—and that Sam deserved more of her. She stood up and slipped her arm around his shoulders so when he straightened and turned to face her, it seemed inevitable their lips would meet.

'I'm so sorry, Sam,' she murmured, feeling the words as they brushed across his lips.

He didn't answer, but drew her close, taking solace, she hoped, in the warmth of her body as it pressed against his. Then the kiss deepened, and desire sneaked in to overwhelm the comfort and compassion that had been on offer. Desire fanned the embers of need deep within Meg's body, setting them alight so heat raced through her blood.

'Sam?'

His name, whispered softly against the corner of his mouth, asked a thousand questions, but Sam had no answers for any of them. All he knew was that he was kissing Meg again, and somehow things might be coming right between them.

He pressed his lips against her eyelids, first one, then the other, kissed her nose, and let his tongue explore the curling lobe of her ear.

She shivered in his arms, then said his name again, only this time it was a command, not a question.

A command to let her go. Turning, he saw

why. The door was open and although the nurse who'd gone for coffee was apparently chatting to someone in the corridor, it would be only a matter of moments before she came in.

Reluctantly Sam released his captive and stepped back, then felt a wave of what could only have been embarrassment wash through his body.

Had he really been kissing Meg right here in the hospital?

Kissing her with fire and passion?

Kissing her in a way that could lead who knew where?

'You should go,' she said, sliding past him and sinking back down into the chair.

'You won't come?'

Stupid question! He'd known that even as he'd asked it—well before he saw Meg glance towards the sleeping Benjie then lift her eyebrows.

He shook his head at his own stupidity, touched her lightly on the arm and left the room.

Left Meg with more confusion in her head and heart than she would have believed possible.

The kiss had distracted her, but before that— even as she sought to comfort him—she'd felt a hint of some question unanswered. A nebulous niggle she couldn't pin down...

Was it just about Sam?

About how all this baggage from his past might have affected him?

She didn't think so, but he certainly had plenty right from the start—a fatherless boy who'd pretended not having a father hadn't mattered. Was she the only one who'd known how much it had bothered him? Known how hard he'd tried at other things, determined to be the best at all he'd undertaken—controlling the parts of his life he *could* control, including his emotions.

Then Ben's words and the gut-wrenching emotional tail-spin they sent him into.

Her mind returned to the kiss—the man's kiss—and she shivered. It had started as a gentle expression of something that couldn't be put into words, then deepened beyond measure, drawing from her a response so different to anything she'd offered or experienced she found herself trembling at the memory.

Forget the kiss—forget Sam!

But she couldn't forget his pain.

Could the Bay heal him as it had healed her?

She'd come back to the Bay to hide away from all the things that had gone wrong in her life, and gradually the place had worked its magic. Eventually she'd found contentment—even a quiet happiness.

Until yesterday, when a tall dark stranger had twirled her panties on his finger…

A gurgle of delight from Benjie woke Meg, who looked around the pre-dawn ward unable to believe she had slept so soundly.

Obviously physical and emotional exhaustion had something going for them!

'Hey, Benjie,' she said softly, bending over the little boy, letting his grasping hands find her forefingers and cling to them. 'How are you doing?'

'I was coming in to ask him the same thing.'

Meg turned to find Jenny right behind her.

'Ben OK?' she asked, and Jenny nodded.

'OK enough to demand I have a shower then come and check on our son. Bossy as always!' She lifted her little boy out of the cot and hugged him. 'Can I slip off his mask and take him through to see Ben?'

Meg looked at the pink cheeks of the little boy nuzzling into his mother's shoulder, and nodded.

'He seems fine,' she said, to confirm the nod, then, as Jenny thanked her for sitting with him, she had to admit she'd done little more than sleep beside him.

'But if he'd woken, he'd have seen you there,' Jenny pointed out. 'He's used to having one of us beside him in the chair, or Mum, if there's a crisis at the farm. So even if you were sleeping, he'd have been reassured. We could probably put a big doll in the chair.'

Meg put her arm around Jenny's shoulders and gave her a hug.

'You always know the right thing to say,' she said gratefully, but Jenny shrugged off the praise, then turned to Meg.

'I don't know what to say about Sam's return,' she admitted. 'Ben and I were talking about it earlier. Are you all right with him being here? I know you split up that Christmas but now he's back...'

'I'm all right,' Meg told her, though when she thought about Sam 'all right' was a long, long way off. All wrong was closer to the mark.

Jenny left, and Meg bent to tidy Benjie's cot, knowing she should leave—go home and have a shower, change her clothes, get ready for another day at work.

But what had been her home was now Sam's home…

As if conjured up by her thoughts, he was standing in the doorway, his clean, pressed, ready-for-work appearance somehow magnified by her rumpled, messy state.

'I remembered you had no transport,' he said quietly, as, anxious not to disturb the sleeping children, she walked towards the door. 'Thought I'd come up early and give you a lift home.'

Home! There was that word again. For some reason—was it seeing Sam, or the remembered image of a little boy nuzzling at Jenny's shoulder?—it no longer sounded welcoming.

She ran her hand through her hair, thinking how dishevelled she must look—not a happy thought but a better alternative than considering unwelcoming homes.

'I can walk,' she said to Sam, and didn't need the lifting of his eyebrows to tell him it was a stupid statement.

But that simple facial movement made her cross. That and the fact there was still a worry lingering somewhere in the back of her mind.

And distracting remnants of the heat of that kiss lingering in her body…

'It's only two miles,' she grouched, then she saw the concern in his eyes and regretted the impulse.

'OK, that's a stupid thing to say. Thanks!' she managed, but still ungraciously, so she forced herself to add, 'If I walked I'd end up late for work.'

She followed him out of the hospital, towards the car park, pausing as he stopped next to a dark blue car.

'Are you all right?'

She looked at him, wondering what he was asking. *Are you all right after all the revelations of last night?*

Or are you all right that we seem to be kissing whenever we're alone?

She went with the former and nodded, although now he'd asked she remembered there was something…

'All right enough, I guess,' she told him. 'It was a lot to take in.'

'I meant about the other thing.'

Meg stared at him, then shook her head.

'By other thing, I assume you mean the kiss.'

He nodded abruptly, a slight frown on his face, as if hearing the word had been distasteful.

'For Pete's sake, Sam, it was just a kiss. It's not as if it was something we hadn't done a thousand times before. Why shouldn't I be all right?'

He was still frowning, only his expression now was one of confusion. For a moment it seemed as if he would say something more, but instead he opened the car door and held it for her. She slipped under his arm—too close for comfort—memories of the kiss that had in no way been 'just a kiss' still vivid in her head. Still tingling along her nerves!

Smelling leather and a hint of a clean, sharp aftershave, she sank into the soft seat, seeing wood panelling as he opened his door and the interior light came back on. Even she, who couldn't tell one car from another, knew this meant serious money had been spent.

Relieved to have something to take her mind off the grumpiness she was feeling, she sniffed the air and asked, 'What kind of car is this?'

He turned towards her and she caught the delight in his smile.

'Is this the woman who used to tell me a car was merely a way for getting from one place to another if it was too far to walk?' he teased, and she wanted to tell him not to smile at her—not to tease.

'I only told you that because you were always raving on about this car or that—showing me pictures of the red sports car you were going to buy one day. This car isn't red and it certainly doesn't look like a sports car.'

'Ah, but looks can be deceiving,' he murmured. Something mechanical hummed softly and suddenly Meg could see the morning sky above them, pale blue streaked with pink from the sunrise. 'Convertible. Do you mind the wind in your hair?'

They were driving very slowly out of the car

park so the wind was little more than a zephyr, though on this already warm morning exceedingly pleasant.

She looked at Sam, seeing not the man but the dream she'd left behind so long ago. She may have mocked his yearning for a sports car, but at the same time she'd pictured herself in just this situation—sitting beside him as he drove, the wind sweeping her hair back behind her.

But this wasn't déjà vu—this was real. Sam was real, the car was real and, yes, the car was moving faster and, tangled though it was, her hair was streaming back behind her now.

'I used to daydream about this,' she said. 'Sitting in the car beside you—the wind blowing through my hair.'

He turned towards her and smiled. 'Well, you were the only girl I ever imagined beside me in the red convertible, although I did wonder if the colour would clash with your hair.'

'Is that why you bought a blue car?' Meg teased, feeling more at ease with Sam than she had since his surprise return.

'Maybe it was,' he told her, but he wasn't

smiling now. He was looking at the road ahead and frowning—just slightly, but enough for Meg to know the moment had passed.

He couldn't possibly have bought a blue car because it would go better with the hair of someone he hadn't seen for thirteen years, Sam told himself. No, not even subconsciously.

But the thought had rattled him—the way just about everything to do with Meg was rattling him.

What had happened to the cool, mature, always-in-control Sam that had been his persona for the last however many years? Where had that Sam gone, and how could he get him back?

He sighed then realised Meg was talking to him.

'How's your mother?'

It was the only thing Meg could think to ask to snap her out of the little bubble of delight that riding with Sam in the convertible was spreading around her.

'She died a month ago.'

Well, that worked! The crisp, matter-of-fact reply was like a slap across her face, and she turned towards him, her lips opening to ask how or why, but his face was set—his profile so stern and hard it could have been carved from marble and hung about with 'don't go there' signs.

In spite of a momentary softening only minutes earlier, he was still adept at hiding his emotions.

But how could she not pursue it?

'I'm sorry. I liked Gina. She was always kind to me.'

'She was kind to everyone.'

A second slap, but Meg realised he hadn't meant either of them to hurt her, his harshness nothing more than reaction to his own pain. Typical Sam, shutting himself off from anything emotional—Mr Tough Guy!

Without thinking, she reached across and rested her hand on his thigh—lightly, but not so lightly she didn't feel him flinch.

Hurt again, she removed it as swiftly as she could, and hid a sigh of relief as he pulled up outside the cottage. She fumbled against the un-familiar door for the catch, desperate to get away from him before she made any more mistakes.

He got out, coming around the car to hold her door for her, silently polite.

What to say? Meg wondered.

Nothing! That's what. No words could cure the pain of a loved one's death. She, of all people, knew that, and though he'd never in a million years admit it, his mother's death must have devastated him. So she nodded her thanks to him for the little courtesy, then found voice to thank him for the lift, and without looking back to see the car move on to the house next door, she made her way to the cottage, calling to her cat as she went, needing something to hold—something to love.

Unreservedly.

The cat, of course, wasn't home.

'You're in the wrong house,' Sam said to the cat who sat, tail curled around his legs, on the kitchen window-sill. The cat blinked its incredible blue eyes—just once—then continued to study Sam, obviously considering *him* the intruder.

But the cat gave him the excuse he needed. Not that he was going to let Meg slip beneath his emotional armour again, but he'd been plain rude to her earlier.

He crossed the room and lifted the animal into

his arms, then carried him down the back steps and across to the cottage.

When Meg opened the side door to his knock, she had already taken off her crumpled clothes and was hastily tying a vivid red, brightly flowered, satiny-looking robe around her body.

It was the kind of fabric that begged a man to run his hands across it—feeling the silky softness, feeling the body beneath.

He knew he must be frowning as this Meg and his Meg had collided in his mind with devastating effect, but remembered just in time why he'd come, and offered her the cat.

'I thought you might be looking for him.'

Duh!

'Thanks,' she said, taking the animal into her arms and snuggling her chin against the furry, dark-chocolate-coloured head.

The cat was an excuse, Sam reminded himself, but he was mesmerised by the lithe, red-clad woman in front of him—by the shiny wrappings, by the body they did little to conceal.

'I...er...'

'Was there something else?'

Did she not know how sexy she looked?

Of course she must!

Why else would she own such a garment, except to put it on for a man?

For the question-mark man?

He peered beyond her, wondering…

'You?' she said helpfully, and he concentrated on the cat to distance himself from other thoughts.

'I'm sorry I spoke as I did in the car. Mum liked you, too. A lot.'

He brushed his hand across his head, kneading at his scalp through the thick, cropped hair.

Why were emotions so difficult?

'It's just still very—recent, Meg. Mum's death.'

Then, afraid if he stayed—if he said one more word—too much might come tumbling out, he turned and walked away, resolutely not looking back, not wanting to see the woman in the red robe, the woman with a cat in her arms.

Meg watched him go and shook her head, sadness overwhelming her. Sadness for Gina, who'd been too young to die, and for Sam, who obviously felt her death very deeply but couldn't—

or wouldn't—talk about it. Couldn't, most likely, unless he'd changed a lot in thirteen years.

But she had no time to brood over Sam's reaction to his mother's death—she had to shower and get to work…

CHAPTER FOUR

'I WANT to see you in my office here on Thursday,' Martin Goodall, the cardiologist, told Ben when he'd finished his examination and agreed Ben could go home, but only if he rested indoors—no work, no stress. 'We'll do some more tests and get you started on a programme of diet and exercise, and don't bother arguing because I've met your charming wife and I'm quite sure you don't want to leave her on her own any time soon.'

Meg smiled to herself as she watched the resentment and denial on Ben's face change to shock. Martin's blunt words would probably do more good than all the nagging Jenny had been doing over the last few years.

She was talking to Martin about another patient he had in the hospital when Sam appeared.

'Dr Goodall!'

Martin frowned at the man in front of him.

'I'm sorry—I don't remember...'

Sam thrust out his hand.

'Sam Agostini. My mother, Gina, worked in your office.'

'Gina Agostini,' Martin said softly, then he studied Sam for a moment before adding, 'So you're Sam. Didn't end up in jail after all?'

There was a dry humour in the words but Sam obviously didn't catch it.

'You're only the fifth person to say that to me since I came back,' he snapped. 'That's the trouble with small towns—everyone's mind runs along the same lines.'

'You did give us cause to wonder,' Martin reminded him. 'How's your mother?'

Sam's face cleared of expression once again and his voice was even as he answered. 'She died a month ago.'

Martin shook his head. 'I'm sorry to hear that, Sam, and sorrier still for the crack I made about how you'd end up. She was a good woman—a wonderful woman. Was it her heart?'

Sam nodded, while Meg, feeling the agonised

tension in the air, wondered why her heart should still ache for Sam—why she should still feel his pain as if it were her own.

It couldn't be love.

Not after thirteen years.

Not when Sam had broken her heart once already…

And especially not when there was still something about his explanation worrying her—something she knew was important but couldn't pin down, her mind stumbling over the kiss whenever she tried to think about it.

She left the two men where they were, and headed back to her office. Benjie's chemo had been delayed for a week, and her prediction that absent staff would return when they heard Sam was back in town had proved true—though she couldn't honestly put it down to news of Sam's reappearance! But at least now she had time to herself and could begin to catch up on some paperwork, which would achieve two objectives.

One, she'd get it done and, two, being in her office, there was no chance she'd keep running into Sam.

And if she kept busy, all thoughts of love would be banished from her mind.

Though she hadn't counted on Bill.

'Can I talk to you?' he asked, coming in with a tray in his hands and a hopeful smile on his face.

'Of course,' she said, thinking of the chairs she wanted for the other wards—just one for each ward would be a start.

'It's about Janelle,' he said, and Meg struggled to switch her mind from chairs to the young woman from the hospital pharmacy Bill was courting.

'Yes?' Meg said cautiously, then she read Bill's nervousness and beamed at him.

'You've finally asked her?' Meg guessed, and saw the blush rise to stain the fair skin on his cheeks.

'I have, but it's not all good news,' he said, sitting down across the desk and twisting his hands together. 'She really, really likes me, even loves me but she's not sure she's "in love".'

He used his fingers to give the final words inverted commas and looked anxiously at Meg.

'Do you think there's a distinction? And if there

is, do you think marriage can work without people being in love?'

'I don't know, Bill,' Meg told him. 'With my marriage, well, Charles and I fancied we were in love. We were also good friends so we thought we could make a decent go of things, but the moment things got tough our marriage fell apart.'

'But surely if we have a strong attraction between us, and mutual respect for each other, and common interests—won't these things build a stronger base for a marriage than being in love?'

'Much stronger, I would think,' a deep voice said, startling Meg so much she all but dropped her cup of coffee, slopping liquid into the saucer as she put it down.

Sam smiled at the evidence of her reaction and she could almost see the words 'Just a kiss?' in a thought bubble above his head.

She scowled at him as he went on in an easy drawl, 'For all the hype about love, has anyone ever measured it satisfactorily? Ever proved it exists? Scientists can quantify most things these days—but love? No one's worked out a way to prove or disprove it!'

'Don't you believe in knocking?' Meg demanded, ignoring his words as her own reaction continued to upset her. How could Sam walking into her office make her spill her coffee?

How could his smile make her pulse race?

Worse still, how could she feel this way about a man who didn't believe in love?

'I did, but you were both too absorbed in each other to hear me. So what's this all about? Love in the hospital? Is the Bay gossip mill slipping that I've been here more than twenty-four hours and haven't heard a whisper of this romance?'

Blue-green eyes cut towards her—this time 'And you've been kissing me as well!' was written in the thought bubble.

'It's not what you think!'

'It's hardly news!' Bill's protest came at the same time as Meg's denial.

'Well, it sounds very sensible to me,' Sam reiterated, cool as a breeze off the water, 'but right now I'd like some help of a medical kind. I have a roster of visiting specialists—who comes to the hospital on which day—but no information on the various consultants, like if they have rooms in town and when they see patients in their rooms.'

'That's all on file. I'll get the details for you,' Bill offered, but when he walked out of Meg's office Sam didn't follow, remaining just inside the door where he'd propped himself on arrival, watching her with an unreadable expression on his face.

'I did knock,' he said again. 'Who's Charles?'

So he'd heard!

Meg lifted her shoulders in a slight shrug, but inside she was still as twitchy as an exposed nerve.

'Not that it's any of your business, but he's my ex-husband.'

'And things got tough? How?'

'*That* is definitely none of your business. And why are you asking? You were never one for sharing *your* emotions, and from your cynical remarks on love, you haven't changed. Yet you're enquiring into my private life? Why don't you go and get the hospital information you want from Bill, rather than poking your nose in where it's not wanted?'

'I'll ask Bill. He seems to know the Meg story, chapter and verse,' Sam replied, and the temper

Meg thought she'd learnt to control escaped its leash and burst free.

'You will do no such thing,' she said, spacing out each word so he couldn't miss the threat in them. 'As I said earlier, my marriage—in fact, my life—is none of your business, Sam. Now, get out of my office and stay out.'

He went, but only after hesitating for an instant, during which Meg contemplated the advisability of throwing her now cold cup of coffee at him.

She was glad she didn't do it—glad she didn't give him the opportunity to see just how rattled she was. It wasn't just the way the past kept coming back to haunt her, but the way she was reacting to the present-day Sam. Shaking so much she spilt her coffee—how pathetic!

'Known her long?' Sam asked Bill as he obeyed part of Meg's instructions and wandered into Bill's office.

Bill's face betrayed his feeling. His cheeks were suffused with embarrassment, but his smile was full of love.

'I guess you heard more than the bit about Meg's first marriage,' he said. 'I've known her for a couple of years—that's how long she's been working at the hospital. I knew straight away she was the one for me, but she didn't know I was alive. Then one day I went into the pharmacy to check about some stock that hadn't shown up on a stock-take and *she* asked *me* out.'

'Meg asked you out?'

Bill turned a puzzled frown in Sam's direction.

'Meg? No, not Meg, Janelle.' Then his face cleared and he chuckled. 'You thought I was talking about Meg and me, but I was asking her advice about Janelle. Meg's been here four years now. She came right after she finished her degree. I think she'd thrown herself into study as a way to forget about her first marriage breaking up and her baby dying, and then work replaced the study that had been the focus of all her attention. Anyway, after she arrived, we soon became friends...'

Baby dying? Bill was still talking but Sam had lost the thread, his mind too busy with the plethora of emotions Bill's explanation had thrown up. First had come relief that Bill was interested not in Meg but in someone called

Janelle. Jealousy had sneaked in unexpectedly as Meg and marriage had been linked in the same sentence, then the baby information…

Meg had had a baby?

It had died?

Now pity poked its head above the parapet.

What agony she must have been through…

No wonder she'd watched so tenderly over Benjie…

'Sam!'

Bill's voice recalled him to the present.

'These are the files you wanted. Read through them at your leisure then give them back to Katrina—she'll show you where they're filed in case you need them again.'

He didn't want to read files. He wanted to go next door and demand to know just what had happened with Meg's baby and her marriage— to know all the bits of Meg he'd missed.

That was crazy!

He went instead to his office and set the files on his desk, noticing Martin Goodall's was on the top.

Martin Goodall? What had he said that was niggling in Sam's mind? Not the bit about being in jail, he was getting used to that. Something else that had raised a flag…

'Was it her heart?'

That was it. Sam had heard the question and agreed, but thirteen years ago, when his mother had worked for Martin, she'd been fit and healthy.

The faulty valve in her heart had been a recent thing.

Hadn't it?

He worried at the question for a minute, then realised worrying at it would get him nowhere. Martin Goodall consulted at the hospital. Sam would run into him again. He'd ask.

But this neat, logical decision didn't obliterate the sadness he always felt when he realised how little he had really known of his mother.

How little he'd bothered to know?

Read the files!

He glanced quickly through them, picking up background information that would help him when he met the various consultants. Then Sally, his secretary, came in to say the other medical and ancillary staff were waiting for him in the board room—today was 'meet the new boss' day!

She led the way then handed him over to Bill, who introduced him to the other doctors. Meg was there, of course, but she was chatting quietly to another woman. Determinedly not looking at him? Sam shook hands with Pete, an intern whom he'd already met, and Kristianne, a young doctor from South Africa who'd been on duty earlier. Then he met another three, who didn't look much older than the intern. Two were English—more young medicos on working holidays, seeing something of the world before they settled down.

Names again became a blur but Sam managed to sort out most of the positions. The older woman with dark hair was the radiographer, a younger version of her the lab assistant, while a bouncy blonde was the physiotherapist and a well-groomed woman in her forties turned out to be an occupational therapist.

Bill had also gathered four local general practitioners, representatives of the four medical practices in the Bay. Fortunately, though two were old enough to have known him, they didn't seem to recognize him. Or if they did, they had more class than to make the 'Why aren't you in jail?' remark.

Sue poured tea and coffee, and passed around plates of cake and biscuits, while Sam explained that although he was only acting super at the hospital, he was in the Bay for the foreseeable future.

'I'll be running the new private hospital,' he explained. 'The new building up near the mall.'

He sensed a movement at the far end of the table and in a quick look in that direction caught the expression of—despair? horror?—on Meg's face.

'We're looking forward to it opening,' one of the GPs said. 'It will mean a number of the visiting specialists can do day surgery here at the Bay rather than their patients having to travel a couple of hours into town.'

'We're looking forward to it opening as well,' Bill assured him, though he was obviously as startled by this news as Meg was. 'At the moment some of the consultants use our theatre for minor procedures that would be more efficiently done in a day surgery theatre.'

'When do you expect it to open?'

'How many beds will it have?'

'Have you appointed staff already?'

'Who actually owns it? One of the big health delivery companies?'

The questions came faster than Sam could answer them, which was just as well because some of them, especially the final ones, he had no intention of answering. The hospital had been built and was owned by a company—his company to be precise, set up by himself and his mother—but there was no reason for anyone to know that.

Eventually the meeting ended, although the local doctors remained behind, wanting to know more of Sam's intentions as far as the new hospital was concerned, and wanting to assure him again that the facility was greatly needed and would be well used.

Out of the corner of his eye he'd seen Meg depart, her back stiff with indignation, as if his failure to inform her of the real reason for his return to the Bay had been a deliberate slight.

Though when had they had time to talk?

They'd had time to kiss…

* * *

She was already in the emergency department when he arrived in answer to a page.

'This is Riley,' she said, glancing up briefly from where she was suctioning blood and other detritus from the mouth of a young boy. 'He fell off the high bar of the uneven bars and tried to catch the lower one in his teeth as he went down.'

Another glance said, *don't ask,* so he didn't question how such an accident could happen, but turned instead to the X-ray a nurse was slotting into the light-box.

The X-ray showed a distinct crack through the mandible, one of the strongest bones in the body, the crack wide enough to have separated Riley's two front teeth. The maxilla seemed intact, although it appeared his upper teeth had taken a hard enough knock to lose their alignment.

'I don't suppose there's an oral surgeon in town,' Sam said to Meg, although what he really wanted to know was where the other medical staff were, that the director of nursing and the medical supervisor were on duty in the ED.

'Broken, huh?'

Knowing able patients preferred to control

their own suctioning, Meg handed Riley the suction device, showing him how to press the button to start suctioning, then moved towards the door of the cubicle.

'There is an orthodontist who did further studies so he's qualified in oral surgery. He's semi-retired up here but he's still an excellent surgeon. Trouble is, he mainly does private work—and he charges like a wounded bull. Riley's dad's a fisherman. There's no way they can afford to pay.'

'So what's the alternative?'

'Sending him to the city, but he might have to hang around for days before they get a specialist to wire his teeth together and insert a plate to hold the bone while it mends. Then they'll have to go back to have the wire removed—'

She broke away from him to cross to the admittance office, spoke briefly to the girl behind the window, then returned, frowning disappointedly.

'Every now and then we get some emergency money from one or other of the service clubs and use it for stuff like this—paying a private specialist. But the kitty's bare at the moment.'

Then she touched Sam on the arm.

'I can only try,' she said, obviously answering some question she'd posed herself and to which he wasn't party. 'We really called you because there's a woman coming in—she's pregnant with twins and having labour pains. The other medical staff on duty are in Theatre—the visiting surgeon's here—but he needs one of our staff to assist, one doing the anaesthetic and the intern's watching because he'll have to assist before the end of his time here.'

'So where are we with Riley?'

Meg passed him the chart.

'He was given some mild pain relief—liquid paracetamol—at the school, but that's all he's had. I haven't intubated him because his airway seems clear, but you'll have to decide about that.'

Meg smiled at him.

'I bet you didn't suspect being a medical super would include all the fun of the ED!'

She hurried away, this time entering the small office and disappearing behind a cupboard that separated the outer room from a second office inside the ED.

Sam went back into the cubicle, where the

nurse who was attending Riley was wiping blood from his chin, while the lad, who looked about thirteen, tried to flirt with her, in spite of the difficulty he was having forming words.

But as he examined the boy's injuries—Meg was right, intubation could have moved the broken bone and caused more problems—he began to consider whether he could pay the oral surgeon. But if he started doing things like that, where did he stop?

Wouldn't there always be someone who needed treatment that cost money?

'I'm Sarah Jensen, Riley's mum.'

The anxious woman came bursting through the curtain, her face so stressed Sam forgot his doubts. He explained the injury briefly, showed Sarah the X-rays then left her with the nurse and her son and slipped away, following Meg's path to the admission desk, speaking quietly to the woman there, asking her to phone the oral surgeon.

'Meg's already phoned him—he'll look after the boy,' the woman said.

'So you found some money to pay him?' Sam asked, delighted at this outcome, not because he didn't want to pay the bills but because it solved his dilemma of when to give and when to hold back. Although that was something he'd have to consider.

Maybe another special fund, set up like the one from the service clubs…

It was at this stage in his considerations that he realised the woman behind the desk was still talking, explaining something about Meg and money, but what he had no idea.

'The surgeon can operate tonight—as soon as the theatre's free.' Meg whisked back into the department just as a youngish man came in through the emergency entrance, and the wail of an ambulance siren as it came through the traffic lights on the hill told them their new patient was almost here.

A nurse Sam hadn't met came through from the hospital, introducing herself as Annabel Cromer, explaining she was a midwife and introducing the obstetrician, Matt Carter.

Sam waited until the new patient, with Annabel and Matt in attendance, had been wheeled into the trauma room, then returned to Riley's cubicle, where Meg was explaining to Sarah about service club money available for emergency treatment like Riley's.

'Did you lie to that woman about the money?' Sam demanded a little later, catching up with Meg as she supervised the tidying up of the ED. Riley had been mildly sedated and was awaiting his operation in a room close to Theatre, and the pregnant woman had been admitted, although drugs had, temporarily at least, stopped her premature labour.

'No, there is money to pay for it,' Meg told him, though something in her voice made him suspect she was the person providing the money.

'Can you afford to do that kind of thing?'

Innocent green eyes looked into his.

'What kind of thing?'

'Paying for that boy's op,' Sam said. 'It's stupid because you set a precedent and there's no way you can always be coughing up for every poor person who comes into the hospital.'

'It came from the fund,' Meg told him, but the fiery colour in her cheeks gave her away. She must have known, too, for she gave him a defiant toss of her head and added, 'Well, it will. Other people can put money in the fund—it doesn't just have to be service clubs. Sometimes some of the big developers here put in money. Anyone can!'

'Even you?'

She shot him a fierce glare.

'If I wanted to!' Then she weakened. 'Anyway, I'm going to phone some of the developers and the service clubs now. Someone's sure to be willing to kick in some cash for Barry Jensen's boy. It's just that they didn't know we'd run out.'

She strode away, then must have remembered what she'd been doing and had to come back, reminding the nurse to restock both the cubicle supply trolley and the trauma room supplies.

Sam was still standing there and she hesitated, studying him, before saying, 'There's just one other thing.'

'Let me guess,' he said. 'The poor staff have been on duty for hours and hours, standing on their feet in Theatre, and you just wondered if perhaps I've had enough theatre experience to assist in Riley's op tonight.'

His smile was so smug she wanted to slap it off his face, but her temper was back under control.

And having a fresh doctor assisting would be the optimum for Riley.

'You don't *have* to do it. Kristianne wants to specialise in surgery when she goes back to South Africa so she's always willing to do an extra shift, but she will have been in Theatre for seven hours and that's a long stint. The anaesthetist side of things will be OK. All the doctors have some training in it, and whoever's due on night duty will do it.'

'But you'll be there?'

Meg nodded. 'I know the Jensens. After he retired, Dad used to go out on Barry Jensen's boat. It seems only right I should be there.' She threw him a defiant look, then added, 'Besides, I like theatre work and don't get many opportunities to do it.'

His silence made her wary, and she studied his face but could read nothing in it, then he smiled and touched her lightly on the shoulder.

'You were always too soft-hearted for your own good, Megan Anstey,' he said, then his smile widened. 'And more often than not, you dragged me into your rescue schemes.'

His hand slid up beneath her hair and cupped the back of her skull and for a moment Meg thought he was going to kiss her, right here in the bright light of the ED.

But all he did was squeeze her neck then release her.

'My surgery skills might be a little rusty, but I can certainly work under direction from an expert so you've got yourself an assistant. Shall we duck down to the canteen and have a bite to eat while we're waiting?'

Meg was still getting over her reaction to his touch. Though a squeeze on the back of the neck could hardly be called intimate, it had certainly seemed that way, and had left a patch of heat on the skin where his fingers had been.

Having dinner with him seemed a very bad idea.

'I'd better go and work the phones so we've got some money to pay the man,' she said, but before she could escape, Sam caught her wrist.

'Every telemarketer in the world will tell you people hate being called at this time of the day.

They're enjoying their after-work drink or preparing dinner. The man won't want paying tonight, so working the phones tomorrow makes a lot more sense.'

'I might not get time tomorrow.' Meg cringed as she heard the words issue from her lips. Not only was it a pathetic excuse, but they'd come out in a desperate squeak.

And Sam's smile told her he knew them for what they were.

'Come on. It's your duty really, because, although Bill showed me the canteen on my guided tour of the place, I doubt I can find it again—and even if I do, how will I know what's best to eat?'

Caving under the pressure of Sam's words and common sense, Meg led the way to the canteen. She was so confused in Sam's presence it was a wonder she was still functioning normally.

That's if slopping coffee everywhere could be called normal.

While her heart seizing up when she'd seen him in his suit in the meeting couldn't even come close to normal.

Seeing the suit, the pristine white shirt, and a blue-green tie that picked up the colour of his eyes, she'd been mesmerised by Sam as he'd stood in front of her at the meeting—a stranger she knew but didn't know.

Though the Sam she *had* known had been just as good at camouflage—hiding his emotions not behind a suit but behind a couldn't-care-less attitude that had kept even his friends at bay.

Hiding them from everyone but her…

Because she hadn't been a local? Because she had only been there for holidays?

'Likely to be someone prepared to give the money?'

She turned to Sam, aware she'd missed most of whatever he'd been saying, suddenly relieved he'd left off the suit jacket so was back in slacks and his white shirt, as he'd been before the meeting—the tie gone again.

'Are you listening to me?'

She shook her head.

'I keep thinking of how you looked in the suit. Somehow, you in a suit just doesn't jell in my head.'

He grinned at her.

'I'm having the same kind of trouble with some of my mental images of you,' he said, the teasing glint in his eyes suggestive enough to make Meg blush all over.

She barged through the doors into the canteen, thankful they'd reached their destination, then the thankfulness dissipated as she realised she now had to eat with him.

CHAPTER FIVE

EATING dinner with Sam had been difficult—although talking to someone about hospital routine while battling physical reactions to the same someone probably needed a stronger word than difficult. But worse was to come, Meg realised as she slipped into a scrub suit and pulled paper slippers over her shoes.

Operating theatres had an intimacy all of their own. Was it the soft background music, or the desultory chat, or the fact the only part of the others you could see were their eyes, protected by clear glasses but still sending all the messages only eyes could send?

And it proved just as bad as Meg had suspected it would. Because this particular surgeon liked his theatre nurse to pass instruments across the patient, Meg was standing close to Sam. Close enough to feel the heat of his body. Kissing close when she turned towards him to pass him something or ask for direction.

Their gloved hands touched time and time again, and although Meg also felt the touch of the surgeon's fingers as well, those gloves sent no messages along her nerves—caused no distraction.

'We insert a titanium plate in here to hold the bone together,' the surgeon was explaining, while Meg held the tiny screws that would hold the plate in place. 'Although it would mend with the teeth wired to close the gap, it would remain weak at this point, hence the plate.'

He inserted the plate into Riley's gums then indicated to Sam to screw it into the bone. Meg handed him one screw and the small electric tool he'd need to screw it home, then passed him the second screw, wincing at the noise of the tool.

'Great job,' the surgeon said, then prepared to wire the teeth together, finally wiring the lower jaw to the upper one, leaving enough room for Riley to sip liquids—the only nourishment he'd get for the next month.

'He's Barry Jensen's boy?' the surgeon asked, as Sam snipped the last piece of wire.

'Yes,' Meg replied, wondering how an oral surgeon would know the fisherman.

'Is he here at the hospital?' the man persisted.

'He should be by the time we come out,' Meg told him. 'Sarah called him on the boat and he was coming straight back to dock.'

'Missing his night fishing,' the surgeon said. 'Anyway, I'll have a talk to him. Man brings in the best prawns of the whole fleet. Soaks them then cooks them in some way that they're free of grit. I reckon a couple of kilos of prawns every now and then will more than pay my fee.'

Meg was so relieved she could have flung her arms around him and given him a big hug, but it was hardly the time, and she barely knew the man. Instead, she smiled at Sam, and the reflected delight in his blue-green eyes sent ripples of excitement down her spine.

'Good result all round,' he said a little later, when, back in their ordinary clothes, they met in post op where a sleepy Riley was realising just how hard it was to talk with his mouth wired shut.

'He talks too much anyway,' Barry said gruffly. 'Be nice to have a bit of peace and quiet around the place.'

But the fingers he rested against his son's cheek were gentle, and the way he held tightly to Sarah's hand betrayed his dismay at seeing his injured lad.

Meg swallowed hard. What was it with this emotional stuff that kept swamping her? Surely it couldn't all be laid at the door of Sam's return to the Bay!

'Time you went home,' he said, guiding her out of the room with his hand in the small of her back.

He'd been talking to the doctor who had done the anaesthetic, and who would stay with Riley until he was transferred to a ward.

'Everything's fine here.'

Meg let him guide her, relishing the warmth of his hand, although she knew she shouldn't. There was still something bothering her—something she couldn't pin down—but all the early warning systems in her body were on full alert, remind-ing her not to get too close to Sam.

'Walk on the beach?'

They were walking together to the car park and

it had seemed such a natural thing for Sam to ask—a long day followed by a relaxing stroll on the beach—he was surprised when Meg jumped as if she'd been shot and spun to face him.

'With you?'

'Why not?'

She frowned at him.

'I don't know,' she said, sounding as crabby as she used to sound thirteen years ago when she'd been out of sorts over something.

Then she added, 'If we do, I don't want you kissing me.'

Sam hid a smile and held up his hands in surrender.

'I only suggested a walk.'

'I know, but I don't trust you.'

'Or don't trust yourself?'

The scowl she shot at him told him she was still crabby, but she was honest enough to add, 'That, too!'

He opened the door of her beat-up old car for her, then drove home behind her, hoping she'd decided on a walk, wondering if she'd really mind a kiss.

Or two…

But when she'd parked her car in the little carport beside the house, she walked across to where he was getting out of his.

'I think I'll give the walk a miss tonight, Sam,' she said quietly. 'I got a bit of sleep last night, but not enough. Some other time, perhaps?'

Sam opened his mouth to argue then closed it again. She probably *was* tired, but beyond that there'd been something else in her voice. Some nuance that told him Meg was distancing herself from him.

Protecting herself?

If she was feeling half the physical symptoms he was whenever they were together, then he could understand she might be wary.

But might she not want to see where they would lead?

He certainly did…

Inevitably the next day was Wednesday, and although knowing they always followed Tuesdays, Sam was disconcerted by the confirmation of this when he saw Sally's neatly typed schedule on his desk.

Every morning she did that—typing up a list of his appointments and explaining where he should be when, and until today—for a whole two days—he'd been grateful. But today seemed to be entirely taken up with meetings, the first one with the director of nursing.

The same director of nursing who'd closed herself off from him the previous evening, refusing even a guaranteed kiss-free walk on the beach.

But would it have been kiss-free?

The part of him that registered his physical reactions every time he saw her—even in the distance—doubted it.

He shut his mind to the distracting thoughts, though he was aware as he did so that the detachment on which he'd always prided himself didn't seem to be working too well. Refusing to give the matter any more time, he tried to concentrate solely on work. His first meeting of the morning with the DON was so, Sally had written, they could review patient numbers for the week, discuss staff issues, equipment concerns and general 'running of the hospital' business.

And according to the timetable Bill would then

join the pair of them for a working lunch so their needs could be put to him and budgetary matters thrashed out.

Meg came in looking as if she hadn't slept for a month, although the pale blue of the hospital uniforms did little for her anyway.

Mentally, he stripped the uniform away, seeing her in the tiny thong and an itty-bitty bra like one of those in the drawer full of undies he still had in his wardrobe.

His body stirred.

When did keeping someone's undies go from a kind of accident to a fetish?

He *had* to get rid of them!

He had to think work—look at her face!

The dark circles under Meg's eyes moved him to pity, a reaction that annoyed him too much to give in to it.

'Maybe you should have walked—you might have slept better,' he said, although he knew this was totally unprofessional behaviour.

'Telling me I look shocking? Thanks, Sam. My ego needed a boost.'

He considered blustering into some kind of

apology but one look at her face, white and tight, warned him to back off.

'Bad night?'

She sighed and sank down into the chair.

'You could say that,' she said, with a smile so pathetic it caused a little hitch in his heart. 'Debbie Waring—the pregnant woman who came in last night? She gave birth at three this morning. Tiny, premmie twins. When Matt realised she had gone back into labour he phoned the special neonate team and they were here by three-thirty, and had the babies stabilised in humidicribs by four. They flew out shortly afterwards, babies and mum, but they were so tiny, Sam—there's a lot of doubt…'

She brushed a hand across her forehead as if to clear away her emotions, and though Sam longed to speak—knew he should—his own emotional reaction prevented it. A reaction caused not by this news about the babies of a woman he didn't know, but by the echo of the news he'd learned yesterday—that Meg had had a baby and that baby had died.

'We can put off this meeting,' he said, when he

finally got his head into order and decided concentrating on work was the best thing to do.

'No way! If I go back to my office I'll fall asleep at my desk then wake up stiff and sore and probably find I've drooled on my notes.'

Sam felt a frown forming on his forehead and willed it away, not wanting Meg to think he was frowning at her. But it *was* at her—or rather at her ability to tamp down her emotions. He'd always been the one who could do that. Meg—well, the Meg he'd known—was more likely to let them all flow out, excitement, despair, whatever. He'd always known what Meg was feeling about something…

'OK,' he said. If she could switch so quickly from personal to professional, so could he. 'Let's meet! From the little experience I have of it, the hospital appears particularly well run. As I'm only here in an acting capacity, I've no intention changing anything, so it seems to me these meetings will mainly be about issues you want to raise.'

That was the little speech he'd prepared before he'd seen her—in fact, he'd prepared it yesterday when Sally had told him the meeting was on today's agenda.

Now he sat back and waited.

And waited.

But when Meg finally spoke, it wasn't about issues and they were right back to personal again.

'Why did you come back?'

He drew in air—hoping she wouldn't notice his chest expanding and contracting—because although it had all seemed so simple, so practical, when the idea had been mooted, now emotional garbage kept coming up and he wondered if perhaps subconsciously…

'I thought we were discussing the hospital.'

The stilted words seemed to make things worse, not better, and Sam gave up all pretence, shrugged his shoulders, walked past Meg to shut the office door, then turned back to face her.

'It was to do with Mum, or at least I thought it was, but now I'm back, I wonder if I didn't have to come anyway, if only to…'

He ran his hands through his hair, aware it was becoming a habit he'd never had before.

'Ground myself sounds trite and stupid, but I can't think of any other way to say it. You accused me the other day of not thinking through my return, and that's not right. I *had* thought it through! But that was back when Mum was alive and it was her dream, not only to come back here but to do some good here. Things worked out that she got some money, quite a lot of money, and she wanted to build a private hospital—I guess if I'd been a teacher she'd have built a school. So, because she'd left the Bay originally because of me and because I owed her in more ways than I can ever tell you, I thought it through and reckoned I could do it.'

'And then she died?' Meg said quietly, and for the first time in weeks Sam felt a lump of sorrow harden in his throat, killing any chance of answering.

So he nodded, but he turned away so Meg wouldn't see his weakness, going back behind his desk and picking up Sally's typed agenda.

'Before I'd finished the administration course I was doing. Before she could get here!'

Another pause, while Meg searched for words

that might ease just a little of his pain, but before she found them, Sam spoke again.

'Which might be why the whole experience has thrown me for a loop,' he managed gruffly. 'Made me vulnerable, I suppose, to the past.'

He looked at her and waved the sheet of paper he still held in his hand.

'Vulnerable doesn't sit well with me, Meg,' he said. Understatement of the year! 'I pride myself on being in control.'

In control—two words and they reminded Meg of what had puzzled her in Sam's explanation of their break-up. He'd been in control—cutting her out of his life with one swift stroke—controlling the break to the extent she hadn't been able to question it—hadn't been able to ask for an explanation.

Why hadn't he talked to her about it? That was the question she wanted—needed—to ask.

But not now, when she was so tired and her heart was still aching for the tiny babies flown away that morning.

Not now when she was, to use Sam's unexpected word, so vulnerable.

Sam was sitting down again—behind his desk— agenda in hand.

'Ready now?' he said, and she knew the time for questioning had passed.

'I guess so,' she agreed, though she wondered if it would be possible to behave normally when the air between them hummed like the wind through high-voltage lines.

'The hospital *is* running well,' she began, when it became obvious Sam wasn't going to open proceedings. 'Though with the flu that's been going around we've been short-staffed, which meant having to transfer two elderly patients to the city.'

'Why elderly patients in particular?' Sam asked, and Meg relaxed. Not entirely, but enough so she could ignore all the Sam-Meg stuff happening inside her while she discussed work-related matters.

'We closed a ward. Well, not a ward in the way you think of a ward, but a two-bedded room. You'll have realised that the kids' ward is the only real ward-type room in the hospital. All the other rooms are singles or doubles, configured in such a way we can have more or fewer patients under each umbrella. So we might have six post-surgical patients one week and only three medical patients, or vice-versa if we haven't had a visiting surgeon for a week. With the absenteeism, we just didn't have the staff to cope with the two elderly patients who were here waiting for accommodation in a nursing home. They're not high-level care, but they do need help, and they really didn't mind being transferred for a week. In fact, I think they looked on it as a pleasant change.'

'Don't regulations mean you can't have patients here indefinitely, even if they are awaiting placement somewhere else?'

Sam's question, more an administrative than a medical one, surprised Meg, although she didn't know why. He'd always been inquisitive, asking why and how and wherefore. No doubt he knew the hospital regulations as well as she did, possibly better if he'd done an administration course.

'Well, they do,' she admitted. 'They limit the number of nights that a patient can stay but, of course, now these two have been away for a week, we can start again.'

She tried a smile and thought he was trying hard not to smile back at her.

'Bending the rules, Sister Anstey?' he asked, allowing a little bit of the smile to escape around the edges of his mouth.

'It's impossible not to!' Meg snapped, more annoyed by her reaction to that faint smile than by his question. But at least she could get rid of some pent-up emotion, because she did think the regulations were all wrong.

'What are we supposed to do with elderly people who have nowhere to go and no family to turn to? Put them out on the street? Give them a refrigerator carton and supermarket trolley to set them up for their new life?'

He smiled properly now.

'That'd be the least we could do,' he agreed. 'And I'm not criticising you for keeping these people here, just wondering if there's something we can do to alleviate the problem in the future. Are there too few places in nursing homes? I would have thought an area like the Bay, where

people have been coming to retire for generations, would be well equipped with retirement
villages, hostels and nursing homes.'

'It is,' Meg said, and sighed. 'There are more
of the damn things than you can poke a stick at—
but nowadays there are entry fees, or you have
to buy your place. How are people who've never
owned their own homes going to pay for a bed
in a nursing home?'

'But means-tested government subsidies exist
—surely they're available for those people,' Sam
protested.

'Of course, but there's a waiting list, and in the
meantime the privately owned nursing homes
and hostels can fill their beds with fee-paying
clients, so why bother taking someone off the
subsidy list?'

Darn it all—she'd got all hot and bothered
again, just when she was trying to be cool and
sensible. And Sam had read her feelings easily,
for he was smiling once again.

'I'm glad you haven't lost your fire, Megan,'
he said. 'It is, and always has been, one of the
most attractive things about you.'

He'd meant it as a compliment, and Meg knew it, but somehow in her head it got twisted up with what he'd had the hide to say earlier—about how terrible she looked.

'Well, that's just great,' she snapped at him. 'You might look awful, Meg, but at least you're fiery!'

'You know damn well I didn't mean it that way, Megan!' Sam glowered at her, jolted out of what had been becoming a dangerous complacency. 'You just looked tired.'

'Well, you weren't afraid of saying exactly what you thought when I came in,' Meg reminded him. 'So why should I imagine you're handing out compliments now?'

Sam held up both hands in surrender, but before Meg could speak again, Bill tapped on the door, then opened it and popped his head in.

'Do come in, Bill, and rescue me before she kills me,' Sam told him.

'You'll need more than Bill for protection,' Meg warned, but she stood up and moved her chair, making room for Bill to join them at the meeting.

But before they could begin again, Sally poked her head around the door.

'Sorry, Meg, but there's an ambulance just come in with a couple of car accident victims so the doctors on duty are flat out, and now we've had a call that there's been a logging accident over on the island. A helicopter's on the way to pick you up.'

'Pick *you* up?' Sam repeated, looking towards Meg who had stood up, excused herself and moved towards the door as if there was nothing strange in the statement.

'I'm a trained paramedic,' she said briefly, and continued on her way.

'But if a doctor's available…' Sam began, following her out the door and along the corridor. 'I don't mean to diminish your ability, but surely if there's one available—'

'You want to come?' she asked, turning towards him. 'Feel free! Four hands are always better than two and, yes, if a doctor is available, he or she will usually go.'

'So you'll go anyway? Even if I'm available?'

Meg continued walking towards the back of the hospital, though she did turn her head and give him a brief glance.

'What do I really know about you, Sam? You're acting super, but a lot of supers don't do hands-on medicine. Have you had recent A and E experience? Have you done helicopter rescues? For all I know, you've been administrating or treating geriatrics or doing anaesthetic work since you finished training. Why would I, or Sally, for that matter, think you'd want to do a rescue flight?'

'You could have asked,' he snapped, glaring down at her, mainly because she was right—she didn't know what experience he had. What he did know was that having inexperienced or untrained staff on rescue flights could often not so much jeopardise the rescue but slow it down.

'I'm paramedic trained,' he said. 'I've recent experience and, as you said, four hands might be better than two.'

The helicopter was waiting for them outside, Simon, the pilot, standing at the door.

'We can land close by,' he said, handing them overalls to pull on over their clothes. 'Ten-minute flight—I'll fill you in on what I know once we're in the air.'

They climbed into the little aircraft and put on the helmets that held the communication equipment they would need to hear and speak.

'There were three men cutting old-growth timber at the top end of the island. They had the chains wrapped around one log ready to drag it out but it was too long or unwieldy, so one of the blokes was cutting it in half when the chainsaw hit the chain and flew out of his hand, cutting his arm. The other bloke reaches out to grab the chainsaw and loses half his hand. The third man gets them both into his ute, thinking he'll drive them out, and in his panic tips the thing over.'

'So who contacted you?' Meg asked.

'The fellow with the injured hand. Used his mobile to dial triple zero. He thinks the driver must have knocked his head and is unconscious and he thinks the other bloke is dead, but as they're all jammed into the front seat of a ute that's upside down by the side of a timber track, who knows?'

Sam felt his stomach squirm at the thought of what lay ahead, but the pilot was telling them to keep a lookout for a clearing in the trees that would denote a timber track.

'He said they had a cleared camp,' Simon added, then he turned the chopper into a low swoop and Sam saw the camp below them. The men had chosen well, right beside one of the beautiful blue fresh-water lakes for which the island was famous. And a nice sandy beach on which the helicopter could land.

'We'll just have to follow the track. The guy said they weren't far from camp. The girl who took the call on triple zero is still talking to him. I've just called in that we're down and on our way.'

The pilot was unloading gear as he spoke, and Sam picked up the biggest of the backpacks, frowning as he saw Meg shoulder one not much smaller, wondering just how often she did this kind of work.

With Simon carrying the third pack, they walked swiftly down the track that led out of the camp, Simon, calling out from time to time, hoping, once other tracks started to diverge, to get a direction from a voice.

Hoping they were in time…

CHAPTER SIX

'HE SAID main track,' Simon told them, as they hesitated once again, then a faint hail from just around the corner told them he was right.

They ran now, knowing they were close, and found the battered old four-wheel-drive vehicle upside down below the level of the track. The cause of the accident was obvious, the sandy road having given way on the bend, taking the vehicle with it, rolling it over.

'Without cutting equipment we need to get it upright or at least onto its side before we can get them out,' Sam said, looking around as if help might come from an unexpected source. But the silent forest offered nothing.

'The helicopter?' Meg asked, looking towards Simon.

'It could provide lift, but to turn it on that unstable ground? I don't think so.'

Sam was lying on his stomach, trying to see in through the windscreen, talking to the man who was trapped but conscious.

Then Meg heard his words and remembered he'd often worked holidays with timber cutters.

'They always have a bulldozer to push tracks and bring the trees out. It's up the road. I'll get it. In the meantime, keep back. The sand's still unstable and the vehicle could topple further.'

'Maybe we could topple it so it turned right way up,' Meg suggested as Sam began to move away from them.

'Have a better look! Maybe it would topple right into the lake if we moved it at all without first securing it to something,' he said, then he jogged off, although she wasn't at all happy at the thought of Sam driving a bulldozer.

What if another bit of road gave way?

What if he was trapped beneath such a huge hunk of machinery?

Don't think about it, she told herself as Simon settled on an old log near the ute and talked quietly to the man or men inside it. Then a rumbling, grinding noise grew louder and Sam appeared, stopping the ugly big machine before the place where the road gave way and leaping out, then unwinding chains from the front of it.

'I don't want to pull it while it's still upside down in case we cause even more injury to those inside, so we'll attach these to the far wheels and see if pulling on them will turn it on its side. It won't be stable but as long as the chains hold, the bulldozer's weight will keep it in place while we get those poor beggars out.'

He passed the end of one of the chains to Simon and indicated where to put it, while Meg shifted the backpacks a little distance away and began to open them up and lay out what they'd need. She put the two lightweight stretchers together, thinking as she did so that the helicopter would have to make two trips.

The noise of the bulldozer's motor starting up made her turn to see Sam raising the big blade at the front of it. As it rose, the chains connected to the vehicle slowly pulled it onto its side.

'That'll do it,' Simon called, waving his hand

in what was obviously a prearranged signal. 'Can you find a way to hold the blade up there?'

Apparently Sam could, and before long he joined them, helping Simon prise open the utility's door.

'Should have tipped it on its other side,' a faint voice said, and Meg had to smile that at least one of the injured men had retained his sense of humour. The man closest to them, the unconscious driver, must have weighed close to twenty stone. He was massive! And now most of his weight was flopped against his unfortunate colleagues.

Sam moved in close, checking that he was breathing, feeling for a pulse, talking to the man but getting no response. But his reflexes showed spinal damage was unlikely so, once they'd secured his neck in a brace, they decided they could lift him out.

'You and what army?' Simon asked, when Sam made this announcement.

'All three of us,' Sam said. 'Meg, you'll have to pull at his legs while Simon and I manoeuvre his body. Simon, if we drop him, we drop him.

The other two are losing blood—we can't delay any longer.'

But, like most things, it was easier said than done. Meg tugged one leg free and then the other, but the two men had a much harder job, getting the man's great belly out from behind the steering-wheel. In the end, Sam pulled off his shirt and twisted it to form a rope, then, using it as a kind of sling, they were able to ease the man off his companions.

Eventually they had him on the ground, and dragged him far enough away to allow them access to the front seat and the other patients.

'Check him out, Meg,' Sam told her. 'Simon, let's lift this other fellow out, then I'll go in and look at the last one.'

Meg checked the big man—airway clear, breathing OK, no bleeding, pulse strong—then she felt around his head, finding a swelling behind his ear. His bulk had stopped him falling forward into the windscreen when the car had tipped over, but he must have slammed his head against the side window. She looked more closely at it. Was there a depression in the centre of the swelling? Linear fracture? With blood matting his hair it was hard to tell—though a skull X-ray would soon show any damage to the bone.

Assuming it was fracture, epidural haematoma was the most obvious thing to look for, but without a scan who could tell?

She lifted one eyelid and then the other. His pupils contracted evenly, relieving her anxiety that there might be pressure already building in his head, causing potential damage to his brain. There was no clear fluid leaking from his nose or ears, but assessing brain injury in the field was largely guesswork. He needed hospitalisation—and soon.

'He OK?'

She turned to see Sam and Simon bending to lower the second man onto the stretcher behind her.

'Swelling behind right ear—possible skull fracture, linear not comminuted. Temporal bone-haematoma is more likely there, isn't it?'

Sam nodded at her.

'Due to damage to the middle meningeal artery. Don't start fluid. We need him in hospital a.s.a.p. so we can monitor him.'

'What's your usual procedure in these cases?' Sam asked Simon, who explained he took acute patients straight to the big regional base hospital an hour's flight away.

'From the look of that chap's hand, and from what we heard about the accident, I might be taking all three of them directly there,' he added, as he followed Sam back to the vehicle, leaving Meg to take care of patient number two.

Meg reached for the packs of swabs she'd laid out earlier and a bottle of saline solution. Blood was streaming from the man's hand, and although his fingers hadn't been completely chopped off, she could see they were badly lacerated, as was his palm.

She refused to look towards the still teetering vehicle, knowing Sam was about to get into it to treat the third man. How had the movement, caused when they'd retrieved the other two, altered the arrangements?

Could the chains give way?

Her stomach tightened but she concentrated on the task at hand.

Literally at hand.

She poured the fluid over the damaged palm and fingers, hoping to dislodge any pieces of dirt or grit.

Simon was right—the hand was so badly damaged there'd be nerve as well as tendon involvement, and fixing nerves and tendons successfully required a skill the Bay hospital medicos, no matter how good they were at surgery, just didn't have.

Knowing it was more important to stop further blood loss than to clean the wound, she padded the damaged hand and wrapped a soft splint and bandages around it to keep the padding in place, then found what she'd need to start a drip. The man was grey and shocky, barely conscious and no longer talking much now the rescuers had arrived. He would need fluid fast.

Wide-bore catheter into his other hand, fluid flowing, Meg started on the other checks—the things that usually came first, but had been ignored because his conversation with them had shown he was conscious and breathing OK. Although she asked him questions and he tried to answer, his voice was hoarse. Choking on the words, he explained they'd all swallowed sand as the vehicle had rolled.

Carefully she checked him over, finding blood soaking through the thick denim of his jeans which, when cut away, revealed more lacerations on his leg. She cleaned them up and dressed them, added pain relief to the fluid he was getting, then began to collect answers from him for the form she had to complete.

Sam called to Simon to help him lift the third man out, and as the two men approached with their burden, the big man moved convulsively.

'Brain injury? Haematoma? Surely not already! How good are you at burr-holes, Megan?' Sam asked, setting his patient down then kneeling by Meg to roll the man onto his side into the recovery position.

His arms flailed, but Meg wondered if it was a seizure, or whether he was simply coming out of his unconscious state.

It seemed to be the latter, for he pushed them away and sat up, then stared at them as if Martians had suddenly landed in his life.

'What's all this?' he demanded, trying to stand up then flopping back down again.

'You had an accident,' Meg explained, moving closer to him so she could check him again, while Sam handled the other badly injured man.

'I never did!' the big man said, and Meg pointed to his vehicle.

'Who drove the bulldozer? Who did that? Who touched my bulldozer?'

Was this an altered mental state?

A symptom of a hematoma—unconsciousness then a period of lucidity?

Was roaring—for he was roaring now and trying to crawl towards his beloved vehicle— considered lucidity?

'Hey, man!' Simon was there in front of him, squatting and talking quietly. 'We needed the 'dozer to get the truck up the right way to get you and your buddies out.'

'Truck?'

The big man shook his head as if to clear it, but the movement must have hurt because he collapsed back onto the ground.

Meg was beside him in an instant.

'Lie still. We'll get you to hospital—get all three of you there. Your mates are hurt. You want to help them, don't you?'

He looked at her and she was relieved to see both pupils were still of equal size, neither of them fixed or dilated.

'You had to use the 'dozer?' he said in a puzzled voice, and Simon explained again, while Meg wondered how they'd ever get him to the chopper on a stretcher—particularly as they only had two.

'You OK with him while Simon and I carry this bloke to the chopper?'

Sam's question answered her own worry. One by one they'd get them there. But could they manage the big man's weight?

She knew the chopper could only safely carry four passengers, three if they were large adults. But that was Simon's problem, she reminded herself.

'Is your head aching?'

The look the man gave her told her how stupid the question was—of course his head would be aching.

'What can you remember?'

Again he looked at her, then the hazy look in his eyes cleared.

'Thommo hit the chain—the chainsaw flipped onto his arm and Joe grabbed at it. Where are they? Are they dead?'

He'd sat up again and, as Meg had no way of stopping him, all she could do was prop her hand against his back so he didn't topple backwards again.

'One of them—Thommo, I suppose—is being carried to the helicopter. Joe's right here. His hand should be OK but we've got to get both of them to hospital as soon as we can.'

'I'll go with them. They're me mates. I've got to go with them.'

He tried to stand but Meg caught his shoulder and he didn't have the strength to shrug her off.

'You can go with them,' she promised him, hoping both Simon and Sam would agree, sure Sam would as it was obvious the man could have a brain injury and would need X-rays, scans and monitoring.

The two men returned as she was thinking of

them, and Sam squatted beside Joe, asking how he felt and did he think, if Meg supported him, he could walk so they could carry the big fellow on the stretcher?

Joe had sat up to assure his mate he was OK, but the big man's roar changed everybody's mind. *He* would walk.

Meg looked from Simon—small, neat and nearly fifty—to Sam, who looked fit and strong enough but beside the big man he was a midget.

'If you walk with him I can carry the stretcher with Simon,' she suggested, and although Sam didn't seem to like the idea he agreed, though it took both him and Simon to get the big man to his feet.

'Should have got him to sign a waiver absolving us from blame if he drops down dead,' Simon said to Meg as they lifted the stretcher with Joe on it off the ground. 'Sam, too! If he falls on Sam he'll kill him.'

'But surely, if he thinks he's well enough to walk, he must be OK,' Meg protested, puffing along in Simon's wake, the soft sand making the job of carrying the stretcher harder than it would otherwise have been.

'I've seen some funny things in the time I've been doing this job,' Simon told her. 'People as conscious and sensible as you and me, walking around and then dropping down dead.'

'Hey, that's my mate you're talking about,' Joe protested.

'He's OK. I think his head's too hard to crack. He was just a bit disoriented there for a while,' Simon assured their patient.

But was he?

Meg didn't know. All she knew was that she was glad Sam had come along. She'd never have been able to manage on her own.

Although…

It was Simon who voiced her doubts.

'You realise I can't take all five of you on this flight,' he said. 'Joe seems the least badly injured, so I could leave Joe and you or Joe and Sam but I don't think the big fellow would like the idea of leaving one of his mates behind, and I need him quiet for the flight. I'll get Sam to give him something to calm him down, then I'll fly the three of them straight to the Bay—that's a short hop and there'll be people there to look after him or help restrain him if he gets stroppy. He can have scans there and if necessary they can put him in an ambulance to take him into town. In the meantime, I can pick up another nurse or medico to travel with the other two to town. Once there, I'll refuel and come back to pick you two up.'

Meg did the sums in her head. Whichever way she looked at it, she and Sam were going to be stranded here for a couple of hours.

Meg peeled off her hot, blood-stained overalls as the helicopter departed. They were back in the first line of trees to escape the whirling sand-storm of the lift-off.

'We've time for a swim,' Sam suggested, and Meg stared at him in disbelief.

'We've no togs, no towels—a swim? Are you crazy?'

'It wouldn't be the first time we've swum in this lake in our underwear, Meg,' Sam teased, though the instant he'd said it he thought of the underwear still residing in his wardrobe at home. Was all her underwear so provocative?

'Yes, well,' she said, colouring deliciously. 'I don't think so.'

'Piker!'

Meg glared at him.

'I'll get burnt.'

'It's four o'clock. The sun's lost its sting, and just look at that cool blue water.'

Wearing the overalls was like being in a sauna and with her uniform made of some synthetic fabric, Meg was sticky with sweat.

The cool blue water of the lake had never looked more inviting. But what underwear had she put on that morning? Which of her cousin Libby's samples had she grabbed out of the drawer? With half of them still in Sam's bedroom, she didn't have much choice, but to take a peak would be a dead give-away.

'I'll go in in my uniform,' she announced. 'Less likely to get burnt that way!'

Sam's look of derision told her exactly what he thought of that excuse, but as he was busy stripping off his clothes and she was getting hotter just watching, she slid off her sensible shoes, removed an assortment of junk from her pocket and ran across the sand to dive into the lake.

It was deliciously cool and, in spite of the hampering effects of swimming in a dress, she splashed around, thoroughly enjoying herself.

Sam stood at the edge of the lake and watched as she porpoised through the water, diving under and coming up again, her wet hair swept back against her skull so the fine lines of her face were revealed.

So, he realised as Meg stood up, was everything else. The wet uniform clung to her body like a second skin and the fabric, formerly opaque, had become transparent, so he could see the black triangles of the bra she wore on her full, high breasts, and the smaller triangle of very skimpy panties between her thighs.

He should tell her.

Embarrass her?

He doubted he could talk anyway. His mouth was dry, his body tense, and his own skimpy jocks would be doing little to hide the rest of his reaction to seeing the veiled delights of Meg's body.

He dived into the lake—cold water should have the same effect whether it was falling on him or he was falling into it!

He swam hard and fast, hoping exercise would dampen his desire, and thought it had worked until he finally swam back and beached himself on the shore.

He looked around for Meg. She wasn't in the water, and as he looked along the beach he saw her emerge from the trees.

In his shirt—her sodden uniform dangling from her fingers…

He watched as she spread it over a bush then retreated to the shade, but the image in his mind was of the scraps of black underwear beneath the wet fabric, and the thought of Meg's mature and luscious body beneath his stained and dirty shirt undid any good the swim might have done.

He turned around and sat on the sand at the edge of the lake, his lower legs and feet still in the water.

'Borrowed your shirt,' she said, sitting down beside him, her long legs stretching into the water beside his, for all the world as if they were ten once more—companions and best friends—relaxed and at ease with each other.

On her side anyway!

'That's OK,' he managed, although his mouth was dry again.

Strange when the rest of him was positively salivating over his companion.

'Love your underwear!'

He hadn't meant to say it but fortunately Meg laughed.

'I might just as well have stripped down to it for all the good that terrible uniform did,' she admitted. 'It's Libby's underwear, actually.'

Now, as well as feeling very randy, Sam was confused.

'You're wearing Libby's underwear? Your cousin Libby?'

'Yes. Though it's not actually *her* underwear inasmuch as underwear she wears. Heavens, you remember Libby—she'd make four of me. But she designs underwear and gives me all her samples and mistakes and trial things that she's not sure about. Free underwear. It's not much of a saving but every little helps.'

Sam felt intensely relieved that she didn't buy the underwear for a man, but stronger than the relief was a desire to see it again—to see it on Meg's body—to slowly strip it off...

Then the words she'd said came through the fog of lust surrounding him and he backed up a bit.

'Not much of a saving but it helps? And although you were living in it, you didn't buy your parents' house? Are you in financial trouble? Could I help?'

She turned to face him, studied him a moment, then smiled—but there was no joy in the expression. In fact, it was a smile that could break a heart—if the person on the receiving end had one.

Whatever—it hurt. Hurt so much he put his arm around her shoulder and drew her close.

'Meg?'

He said it as an affirmation of their friendship, but it was still a question.

He waited, watched her profile while she stared out across the lake—then saw a tear slide down her cheek.

'Meg?'

The word was more urgent now, and it seemed to jolt her from her reverie, so much so she brushed away the tear and tried a better smile.

'This morning was difficult for me. Babies get to me,' she said, and stared at the lake again.

'You lost a baby?'

She didn't question how he knew, just nodded, but when he drew her even closer she didn't move away, instead resting her head against his shoulder and letting the words drift from her lips—calm, quiet words, devoid of any emotion.

'She was born with hypoplastic left heart syndrome. Charles—my husband—and I were both first-year med students—we'd done our premed degrees and had three years to go to qualify. We got married because I was pregnant, which in retrospect was totally stupid, then when the baby came and was in such trouble—well, we parted. The doctors in Brisbane didn't want to operate—said she wasn't strong enough for all the ops HLHS entails, but you know me, Sam, stubborn to the last.'

He could feel the pain of her memories wrap around him like a net, and though his arm tightened around her shoulders, he didn't speak. Afraid to break the spell that held them both in thrall—afraid she wouldn't tell him more…

'I had her flown to Melbourne, to specialists at the Children's there.' Whispered words, thick with emotion, thickening Sam's throat just listening! 'She had the operation—a first stage Norwood—but she died six weeks later.'

'Oh, Meg, my love!' Sam turned her in his arms and held her close, pressing kisses on her head as she clung to him while remembered grief, too deep for tears, washed through her body.

They sat together for a long time, holding each other. His own body was suggesting more than comfort, but until Meg raised her head, and those usually clear green eyes looked hazily into his, he'd kept it under control. Her whispered 'Sam?' was both thanks and a request, and he caught the end of his name still on her lips as he kissed her.

The kiss simmered with all the frustration of thirteen long years apart, yet he held himself in check, slowly exploring her mouth, pressing kisses on her skin—temple, eyelids, neck. His hands explored her body, while hers pressed against his chest, then kneaded at his shoulders and dug hard into his hair.

Slowly working lower, his kisses pushed aside his shirt to reach the soft swell of her breast, and the scraps of black lace that imprisoned her taut, peaked nipples. He heard her gasp as he took one in his mouth, teasing around it with his tongue, before suckling gently through the lace—nipping with his teeth.

'Sam!'

Would one word—his name uttered in desperation—tell him she was begging him to continue? Tell him how her body burned and ached and needed him so badly she was shaking with desire?

Tell him only he could wash away her pain?

Only he could bring oblivion…

Something must have worked for he was kissing her again, whispering against her lips. One hand continued to toy with her nipple while the other found its way between her legs, sliding aside the useless black lace to tease and probe and seek that magic place where all sensation met, sliding back and forth until she cried out for release.

'Not so fast,' he murmured, sliding his hand upward over her warm, receptive skin. 'We've waited thirteen years for this, Megan. There's no rush now.'

Wasn't there? Her breasts were throbbing and the ache between her legs made her want to moan in protest, but this was Sam, and two could play at that game.

His jocks were stretched tight across his thighs—soft, silky fabric with enough give in it to encompass a truly tantalising erection. She found it easily, and stroked softly, teasing at the tip until he was moaning, too.

Then she slid her hands around his hips and eased the straining fabric downward.

'Still no rush, Sam?' she teased, as she slid her mouth down his chest towards but one destination. All constraint between them was now gone and Meg revelled in her power, although the power *he* held over *her* body was more than equal to it.

'Still no rush,' he agreed through gritted teeth, nibbling now at the skin on her neck, the two of them so intertwined it was only the stark contrast in their skin colour that told one from the other.

'Meg, you're killing me!'

She smiled in triumph, although he'd cried surrender only seconds before she gave in to need herself.

Turning, she lay back on the sand, drawing Sam on top of her, drawing him into her, needing him to fill all the aching, lonely places she'd carried inside her for so long.

But Sam still held his nerve, teasing her beyond endurance, bringing her to a shuddering climax, before he finally gave in and joined her with a whoop of conquest that must have rung through the ancient forest like an echo from primeval times.

'Oh, dear!'

Meg wasn't sure she'd said the words aloud until Sam shifted, swinging her in his arms so she lay on top of him, and his eyes, the reflected blue of the sky, asked for an explanation.

'Oh, dear?' he repeated, when she didn't answer.

She smiled at him then hid her face on his shoulder.

'Oh, dear, how did that happen? Oh, dear, I didn't know it could be that good? Oh, dear, it's a long time since I've had sex? Oh, dear, what have we done?'

She offered all possibilities, the words muffled against his skin, but didn't voice the real concern—oh, dear, what happens now?

One hand grasped her chin and tilted her face so he could look at her when he spoke.

Or had it been so she could see his smile? The kind of satisfied smile her cat gave her when he'd eaten the steak she'd put out for dinner, although as he looked at her she saw the smile change and remembered.

'It happened because you needed to be held—and maybe I did, too,' he said carefully. 'Because sometimes pain can only be washed away by the expression of love, Meg—by giving and receiving pleasure in the way we've just done.'

He drew her close again and she rested with her head against the crook of his neck, her lips pressing grateful kisses on his skin. Then, a little later, he eased away and cupped his hands around her face.

'As to the rest of your questions, my sweet, I'm pleased about the second one—naturally,' he said,

the smile growing even more delighted. 'And I'm
sorry I wasn't around to help you with the third.'

His arm tightened around her and he drew her
close.

'As to the "what have we done?"—we've made
love, Megan, just as we intended doing thirteen
years ago. And do you know what?'

His eyebrows arched with the question but he
didn't give her time to answer it.

'It was every bit as good as I thought it would
be—no, that's wrong. In my callow youth there
was no way I could have imagined sex could be
that great.'

'Made love'—'sex could be that great!' The
two phrases didn't quite jell.

But he was holding her close again. She was
in Sam's arms—and for a little while at least she
wasn't going to think about anything else.

Until he said, 'The medical bills? They left
you with debts? Is that why Libby's underwear
is a saving?'

She straightened up and shifted so she could
look at his face.

Which told her nothing.

'Why are you asking?'

'I could pay them off.'

It was so absolutely out of left field she couldn't speak. Couldn't think! But she did know there was something very wrong.

She escaped his arm, sat up on the beach and looked down at him.

'You can what?'

He frowned at her, but as his gaze drifted from her face she realised she was naked and he was looking at her breasts, pink from his attentions and the heat of love-making—or sex, or whatever! She stood up, grabbed his discarded shirt and wrapped it around her body.

'Pay them off. I've plenty of money.' His voice seemed to come from a long way off, and she knew he was thinking more of sex than his answer, but that didn't make his offer—or the timing of it—any better.

'I don't need payment!' she told him, and she stalked away, grabbing at her uniform, still damp but wearable, and hurrying towards the trees.

Stupid, she knew, that she should be embarrassed by Sam seeing her body—particularly after what had just occurred, but her thoughts were flapping around like the wings of an injured bird, while her treacherous body had actually responded to Sam's hungry glance.

She pulled her uniform over her head and marched back down the beach to find her underwear, though she doubted whether the flimsy garments had survived their fevered treatment.

Sam was swimming—far out in the lake—naked, apparently, for his jocks were lying on the sand.

Her bra was in one piece, but the lacy thong had snapped one ribbon so she shoved the lot into her pocket and glared out at the swimmer, wondering why his offer had upset her so much.

Because it was Sam taking control again? *You've got a problem, I'll fix it?*

Had he always been the same?

She couldn't remember him controlling her life, but he'd certainly exerted rigid control over his—determined to prove himself at whatever he took on, determined to be the best.

But now? They were mature adults, with all

the baggage that entailed. She with a broken marriage and a dead baby behind her—her debts now paid off but the dream still to be funded.

He with—heaven only knew.

He'd turned and was swimming back towards her, cutting the water with long, clean strokes, the Sam of her past morphing into the man who'd made her body tingle, throb, burn and exult—all in the space of minutes.

He stood up and marched out of the water— totally unembarrassed, not hiding his nakedness as she had done. Her eyes feasted on him, taking in the muscle beneath the tanned skin, taking in the paler skin above his thighs—taking in Sam in all his naked glory.

And her body tingled, throbbed and burned all over again so it was only the beat of the returning helicopter's rotors that stopped her casting herself into his arms, apologising incoherently for making things go wrong again between them and begging him to put them right.

With sex!

Was that all it would be?

He was pulling on his jocks, as silent as the lake

itself, then he straightened and acknowledged her presence with a nod.

'Put my shirt on over your uniform,' he said carefully. 'The material's still too wet to hide much!'

Meg bent and picked up the wet, dirty shirt and with trembling fingers wrapped it around her body, then he was there behind her, taking the shirt, holding it so she could slide her arms into it.

Holding her…

She had to say something, but words wouldn't come, and now the helicopter was so close they had to move into the trees, she towards the closest grove, he back to where they'd taken off their clothes earlier.

The noise had made speech impossible, even if Sam had been able to think of something to say. Heaven had been in his arms and while his common sense might scoff at such a smarmy thought, that's how he had felt, lying on the beach, holding Meg.

Then out of his mouth had come words that he'd meant as—not payment definitely. Just something to help her out. Some kind of…

Reward?

Wasn't that as bad as payment?

Hell, he had no idea what he'd meant except to help her—to do anything he could for her because…

Because he loved her?

What did he know about love? He who had guarded himself against all emotion, knowing it weakened resolve and led to vulnerability?

No, love was nonsense.

He pulled on his trousers, gathered up his shoes and both sets of overalls, watching the sand churn up as the helicopter landed, watching Meg run from the trees as the rotors slowed and Simon opened the door.

She didn't put on a helmet so he couldn't ask her on the flight, and once back at the hospital she disappeared inside so quickly he didn't know where to look for her. Not in her office, because he had to pass it to get to his and hers was definitely empty.

'Oh, dear, you've lost your shirt.'

Sally's response to his naked chest made him smile, but it also reminded him he hadn't brought any spare clothes to the hospital.

'Can you find a scrub suit for me—just a top will do—and is there somewhere I can shower? I had a swim while we were waiting for the helicopter to come back and although it was fresh water, my feet are sandy.'

She led the way to the medical staff locker rooms—part of the hospital he'd missed in the guided tour—then returned seconds later with one of the flimsy blue tops staff wore in the operating theatre or when doing messy jobs. She opened a cabinet to show him where clean towels were kept, then left.

Was Meg showering in the nurses' locker room? he wondered as he stood under the streaming warm water, seeing not his own body but her pale curves and long shapely legs. His body stirred again and he knew he had to make things right between them. Right enough for what had happened on the beach to be the start of something, not the end.

CHAPTER SEVEN

'I'M TAKING you out to dinner tonight. We need to talk.'

Meg, showered and clad in clean jeans and a T-shirt which were the only spare clothes in her locker, looked up at the belligerent man who stood just inside her doorway. The blue scrub shirt, like the sky had earlier, made his eyes seem bluer, a distracting thought she really didn't need right now.

Especially as her body warmed with remembered love-making—remembered delights she didn't want to think about.

But she supposed they did have to talk if they were to continue working together in anything other than a state of tense truce. They could hardly ignore what had happened between them that afternoon. Though that didn't mean she had to take orders from him.

'You could ask nicely,' she suggested, and saw anger spark in his eyes before he realised just how his demand had sounded.

Then he smiled.

'OK,' he agreed. 'Please, Meg, will you have dinner with me tonight? Where's a good place to eat? What about Lumiere? Is it still operating down by the beach?'

She hid her own smile as she said, 'That would have worked better if you'd waited for my answer before asking about venues but, yes, Lumiere is still operating and still serving the best food in town.'

'Get taken there a lot, do you?' he said, and although he smiled to pretend he was just teasing, Meg wasn't sure.

She wasn't sure about anything right now.

He couldn't possibly be jealous—so why say it?

She couldn't ask because he'd disappeared again, so she contented herself with a low growl of dissatisfaction at the whole situation.

Back to work! She lifted the phone and rang the regional hospital to enquire about the patients from the island. The third man, Ian Thomson, was being prepared for an airlift to Brisbane, the local surgeons doubting they could save his arm, but Joe was currently in Theatre and the big man, Harold Harvey, transported there by ambulance at his own insistence after being examined at the Bay, was resting, though not, the nurse told Meg, quietly.

'Glad he's yours, not mine,' Meg said to her, and the man on the other end of the phone chuckled.

She tried to concentrate on the letters and files that had piled up in her absence. Wednesday was the one day of the week she always spent on office work, and even on Wednesdays when she hadn't been called for rescue duty, she rarely finished all she had to do on time. So it was close to seven when Sam gave a perfunctory knock and came in.

'We're going out to dinner,' he reminded her.

She was nearly finished the next fortnight's rosters so she nodded without looking up.

'Your car's not in the car park.'

'My car wouldn't start so I walked to work.'

'You could have asked me for a lift.'

Meg lifted her head and looked at him. The physical pleasure they'd shared should have brought them closer—or at least eased the quivering sexual tension that had been simmering between them. But that part, as far as Meg was concerned, had grown stronger. She wanted to fling herself into his arms and stay there for ever.

As for being closer—as friends or colleagues— somehow they'd mucked that up again!

'I often walk, Sam. It's no big deal.'

She spoke gently, not wanting to make things worse, but couldn't tell from his closed expression what he was feeling.

'I'll drive you home.' Hardly a gracious offer, but one she was about to accept when he added, 'You *do* want to go home, don't you?'

There was a growl hidden in the words but before she could ask what on earth was wrong he added, 'Maybe put on some underwear.'

She glanced down to see the two bumps of her nipples showing through the T-shirt, but refused to let her embarrassment show.

Refused also to get into another argument with him.

'Go away, Sam, and let me finish this. I'll be ready in fifteen minutes. And I'll put on more than underwear,' she muttered to herself. So far he'd seen her in her unflattering uniform, her daggy old shorts, covered in blood—

She'd show him!

Lumiere was nestled at the base of the steep slope that rose up from the beach to form the next bluff along from the Point where Sam and Meg lived. He had walked past it often enough to know the outside tables were nestled beneath pandanus palms on thick grass that spread right to the edge of the sand. With the moon still pretty full, and a clear cloudless sky, he'd asked for one of these tables, thinking at least the setting would be romantic, even if his proposal wasn't.

Not that Meg would expect romance. She was as practical as he was. But practical or not, the idea was generating a modicum of excitement in his belly as he walked next door to collect his 'date'.

Weird, this, when he'd always walked the other way before…

The side door was open and he called out her name then wandered in, seeing familiar Anstey furniture in what had been his home.

Finding it didn't look out of place.

'I'll be a minute,' Meg said, slipping from the bathroom to the front bedroom that had always been his mother's. But it wasn't his mother he was thinking of, it was Meg, and the body he knew lay beneath the red robe she had wrapped around it.

Sex before dinner?

It needn't take long.

He was considering following her into the bedroom when she reappeared, wearing what he supposed could be called a dress, though it showed far more of Meg than it covered.

'Zip me up, would you, Sam?' she said, turning her back to him so he could get to a minuscule zip that pulled the dress together across her buttocks but left most of the rest of her back bare.

And pearly white against the dull sheen of the fabric.

Translucent white.

No bra.

His breathing had hitched somewhere deep in his lungs, and he grabbed a gulp of air before leaning forward to press a kiss against that bare, pearly whiteness.

'And another catch here,' she was saying, her hands holding her hair away from her neck and at the same time poking two pieces of fabric towards him.

He forgot the kiss and forced his glazed eyes to find the tiny hooks and eyes that would hold this creation together at the top. But no sooner had he achieved this miracle than she waltzed away, returning a minute later with her feet thrust into strappy black sandals with heels high enough to make a diving board.

'OK?' she said, not asking for a comment on how she looked but rather suggesting they should go.

He didn't answer, simply staring at her, unable to believe that this was Meg.

His Meg.

By heaven, she'd better be his, because, there was no way he could cope if she was anyone else's.

'You look beautiful,' he said when her fine eyebrows had gathered in a puzzled frown at his lack of movement.

'Surprised, Sam?' she teased, though he could see a glow of colour in her cheeks. 'Didn't you ever read the story about the ugly duckling turning into a swan?'

'You were never an ugly duckling,' he argued, still drinking in the slim but shapely figure in the scrap of black fabric, the swell and shadow of cleavage in the deep V of the neckline—her breasts apparently held up by magical sky-hooks. Tiny waist then the legs that stretched from a skirt apparently made up of black hand-kerchiefs, caught here and there by a corner, so the hemline was a series of points and the white legs flashed between them whenever she moved.

'Shall we go?'

Had he stood staring for too long that she felt she had to ask? He gathered his wits as best he could, looked at her shoes and said, 'I'd thought we'd walk but maybe I'll get the car.'

'No way. I can walk in these. They're just sandals with a bit of height.'

She leaned over the armchair and picked up a tiny handbag and a long length of fabric that seemed to have been sewn with precious stones. She threw it carelessly around her shoulders and he saw it was a fine shawl with a peacock pattern on it, the peacock feathers picked out in the flashing stones.

'You're beautiful,' he said again, aware it was getting a bit repetitive but unable to hold back the words.

This time she accepted the compliment with a gracious smile and led the way out the door, but as Sam followed he began to worry, began to be less confident that getting Meg's agreement to the idea he'd had—there on the beach beside the lake—just might not be the cakewalk he'd assumed it would be.

The satisfaction that she'd stunned Sam with her 'dressed-up' look kept Meg quietly amused for the first part of their walk along the Esplanade. He'd seen her at her very worst earlier today, wringing wet and wearing his dirty shirt, so pride had insisted she go all out tonight. The dress was one she'd picked up in a 'second time around' shop to wear to a formal function years ago, and she knew she always looked good in it.

But as they made their way down the road that led to the beach and the restaurant, she began to wonder if it had been such a good idea. Sam responded to her polite attempts at conversation, but it was obvious his mind was elsewhere, though not, she thought, on the sexual tension that still sizzled in the air between them.

In the end she gave up, delighting instead in the smell of the eucalypts in the salt air and the bright path of moonlight stretching across the calm waters of the bay.

Lights like Chinese lanterns illuminated the gardens of Lumiere, although tonight, with the moon's effort and the moonlight reflected off the bay, they were more decoration than necessity. Sam gave his name to the youngster who met them at the door, and together they followed him to a table by the beach. Later on, when the tide rose, they would have water there at the edge of the grass. Water and moonlight—she'd been right about it being too romantic.

Romantic was confusing…

'Champagne for madam, too?'

Meg turned from the young waiter to Sam, then back to the waiter. She must have missed Sam's order.

'Definitely champagne,' Sam answered for her, and though she wanted to tell him that champagne would give her a sinus headache in the morning, she was unsure enough about the situation not to argue, although she did ask for water as well and a glass of ice, so she could drop cubes into the champagne to water it down.

'This is lovely,' she said, looking around the garden that surrounded them, 'but a bit of overkill, surely. I know we have to talk, but we could have ordered pizzas and talked on your veranda.'

She'd been trying to kill the romance that was sneaking all around her, and from the frown on Sam's face she'd succeeded.

'Well, I know what I want to say is more practical than romantic, but I thought the setting might be…well, special.'

Special to soften the practicality? Meg wondered as the waiter returned and went through the procedure of opening the champagne without popping the cork too loudly. What practicality?

What happened happened, so let's forget about it and get on with our lives?

Or maybe, *The sex was great, so why not keep*

doing it? Any reason why not? That kind of practicality.

The waiter poured a little champagne for Sam to taste, hovered while it was appreciated, then poured them each a glass.

Getting more nervous by the moment, Meg barely waited until his back had disappeared into the shadows before asking, 'And what *did* you want to say, Sam?'

'Let's order first,' he suggested, passing her a menu.

Did she want to have an affair with him, if that's what he suggested? She was thinking about that rather than mussels in a chilli sauce.

He was only at the hospital for a month—rack of lamb was always a good choice—and once he left it would be less awkward than having an affair with a colleague.

'Do you want oysters first?'

Aphrodisiacs—or so people said. The pair of them hadn't needed them that afternoon.

She shook her head and when he said, 'Some other appetiser perhaps?' she realised he'd taken her headshake as an answer.

Concentrate on the menu, order a meal, then ask the question again.

'I'll have the stuffed mushrooms and the Thai beef salad.'

There, that was done. The waiter reappeared, Sam gave the order—for him the oysters and rare steak. They'd be making love all night! Meg's stomach gave a little flip of excitement at the thought and parts of her that had already registered extreme pleasure that day warmed with anticipation.

She really had to stop thinking about sex.

'So, what did you want to say?'

'Heavens, all we're doing is having dinner together—do you have to keep nagging about what I wanted to say?'

'I've only asked twice, and you did say you wanted to say something, but you keep putting it off with drink orders, and oysters, and dinner orders.'

'We're here to eat and drink,' he reminded her, lifting his glass and holding it out in front of him, waiting for her to raise hers and touch it— waiting for a toast.

But for what?

Meg slid an icecube into her champagne, then raised the glass and touched his.

'Welcome back to the Bay, Sam,' she said.

'Thank you,' he said formally, and they both sipped, Meg taking enough so she could add another icecube.

If Sam had any objections to what she was doing to his hundred-dollar-a-bottle champagne he didn't mention it, although she was sure the waiter, who was walking past at the time, flinched.

Meg took another sip, mainly so she wouldn't ask him what he wanted to talk about a third time, but this dithering wasn't like the Sam she'd known as a child. That Sam had usually come right out with things. Oh, he'd thought them through first, but once he'd made a decision about something, that had been it.

'I think we should get married.'

OK, it wasn't any of the things she'd thought he might have decided, but at least now it was out in the open.

Was she thinking that because the content of

the sentence was so unbelievable she didn't know *how* to think about it?

'You think we should get married?'

Suddenly a whole lot of stuff came bubbling up.

'Just because we had sex on the beach, you think we should get married? Are you mad, Sam? We hardly know each other. We might have been childhood friends, but thirteen years is a long time—it's our whole lives as grown-ups so far. We mightn't even like the people we've become. Anyway, I don't want to get married.'

Fortunately, before she could enlarge on that or release all the other reasons his suggestion was impossible, the waiter appeared with their first courses.

Meg waited until he disappeared again then grinned at the dozen oysters nestling in their shells on Sam's plate.

'That doesn't mean to say those will be wasted,' she told him. 'I'm perfectly willing to have an affair with you.'

'And what if I don't want an affair?' he growled, poking at the oysters as if they were the last things he wanted to eat.

Meg hid her disappointment.

'Well, that's OK as well. It would have been kind of awkward while we're both working at the hospital anyway. Quick cuddles in the storeroom—that kind of thing.'

'I have never resorted to quick cuddles in a storeroom,' he said stiffly, finally raising an oyster to his lips.

'Never wanted someone so badly you couldn't wait?' Meg teased, slipping one foot out of its sandal and lifting it to rub her toes along his leg—up and up until it raked along his thigh. 'Never needed just a kiss?'

He was staring at her as if she were a total stranger, but he hadn't stopped her foot's exploration of his thigh and she knew he was feeling the physical electricity sparking between them again, as strong as the power from high-voltage wires.

'Never,' he managed, but the words were choked out. She relented and moved her foot back into its proper position under the table—but not into its sandal in case it was needed again.

'Poor you!' she murmured sympathetically, not sure why she was teasing Sam this way but enjoying every minute of it. For one thing, it took her mind off his stupid declaration.

Which *was* stupid, although her heart had all but stopped beating when he'd made it.

The waiter appeared to take their dishes away, realised Meg hadn't begun hers and Sam hadn't got further than his first oyster, and backed off.

They ate in silence, but their conversation left a bitter taste in her mouth and the mushrooms, which Meg was certain were delicious, now tasted like sawdust.

Sam finished his last oyster and pushed his plate away.

'Why don't you want to get married?'

Meg hesitated, then went for an easy way out.

'There's a lot I want to do.'

'And marriage would stop that?'

She frowned at him, unable to believe they could be talking this way.

Or *he* could be talking this way! She was too flabbergasted to say anything much.

'I wouldn't stop you doing anything you want, Meg. You know that. But look at it from a practical point of view. The physical attraction between us is still strong and we like and respect each other and we have our shared past. Surely when you add it together, it makes an excellent basis for marriage.'

Meg stared at him, and although in a way it sounded exactly like Sam—planning their lives as he'd always planned the activities during their holidays—to leap from one sexual encounter straight to marriage was just too much!

'Have you gone mad? You're talking nonsense. What do we have between us—apart from today by the lake?'

'You said yes last time I asked you to marry me!' he growled. At least now he was showing some emotion. 'You used to write "Megan Agostini" in the sand.'

'That was thirteen years ago, Sam!' she reminded him.

'And you're saying we've changed fundamentally since then? That if what happened hadn't happened—if we *had* married young—we'd be divorced by now?'

Megan flung down her napkin and stood up.

'I'm too hungry to walk out on you,' she told

him, 'and too angry to sit and listen to your nonsense. I'm going for a short walk on the beach. I'll be back in time for the main course.'

She kicked off her other sandal and strode away from him, trying to make sense of his behaviour. It had to be the sex that had prompted this marriage thing. Although maybe it was to do with his mother? Was he aware of whatever she'd had to live through as a single woman raising a child? Possibly! But he was thirty years old— and an incredibly sexy man—so he must have had affairs with other women without insisting on marriage.

She hooked her hair behind her ears and looked up at the moon, then turned and walked more slowly back again.

'Why marriage, Sam?' she asked as she approached the table, but right on cue the waiter appeared again, bearing their main courses. He fussed around, filling their glasses, shifting cutlery, flicking at non-existent crumbs with a napkin.

Had he heard enough of the conversation to be interested in what happened next, or was he just another aggravation in her life?

Sam didn't seem concerned, cutting into his steak and sighing in satisfaction as the blood oozed out of it.

'Eat your dinner!'

Sam back in bossy mode.

Taking control…

Meg ate, and enjoyed the meal, but she was waiting for an answer and intended to get one before they parted back at the cottage.

The beef salad was delicious, hot and spicy yet cool as well—a bit like Sam, really.

'Something funny?' he asked, and she tried to remove the smile that had escaped.

'More ridiculous than funny,' she assured him, certain he wouldn't like being compared to a beef salad.

'Well, I'm glad you're enjoying yourself,' he muttered, then he turned his attention from his almost empty plate to her, his eyes, shadowed by the light behind him, looking intently at her but giving nothing away.

And though she'd managed to get through the evening so far with levity and smart remarks, Meg felt unease increase inside her. She reached for another icecube for her drink, though in reality it was her skin that needed cooling.

Sam caught her hand and held it, his fingers slipped into her palm, stroking and kneading.

'Did he hurt you so much, your first husband, that you don't want to marry again?'

It was the last question she'd expected him to ask—so much so she had to think for a moment before answering.

'Charles? No, he didn't hurt me. Or I him, as far as I could see. Getting married was the bad idea and when we had the baby he was far more sensible than I was about it. I called her Lucy.'

Sam could see her heart beating in her chest and feel her pulse rate rise in the wrist he now held when she talked about the baby, and knew she still felt pain too deep to measure.

But how to help her heal? How to make Meg whole again? In her mind marriage and babies must be linked—for surely that must be the reason she'd laughed off his proposal.

But she'd given him a gift, her baby's name—Lucy…

'So, you see, although eventually I'd like to

marry and have more children, right now marriage really doesn't come into my plans.'

She gave a satisfied kind of nod and removed her hand from under his, but he'd obviously missed a huge part of the conversation.

'Because of babies?' he hazarded, going with what was uppermost in *his* mind.

'Babies? We weren't talking about babies—we were talking about why I wouldn't marry you.'

'And it's not because of babies?'

'Just how much of the champagne have you had to drink? Or do you just not listen to anything you don't want to hear?'

She wasn't angry, but stirred up enough to have brought colour to her usually pale cheeks, and she was so beautiful he could only stare at her.

And remember...

Not the distant past this time but the recent past—that afternoon...

And she'd not been averse to an affair.

In fact, she'd suggested it...

'Let's talk about it later,' he said, shoving back his chair and standing up. 'I'll fix up the bill on the way out.'

'No coffee with a little chocolate on the saucer?' Meg raised her eyebrows but she was standing, too, and bending to pick up her sandals.

He remembered the way her foot had teased and his control wavered, but he took the delicate straps from her hand to carry them, and put his free hand on her bare back to guide her towards the exit.

'Later,' he whispered in her ear, bending forward to brush a kiss on her white shoulder. 'Chocolate, coffee, anything madam desires, but much later...'

They walked home, arms linked behind each other's backs, not daring to stop and kiss because the tension sizzling between them was enough to know that one kiss would ignite too much heat to control and making love on the Esplanade wasn't much accepted in the Bay.

They dithered only momentarily outside the cottage, and Sam's 'My bed's a kingsize' won. But once inside his bedroom, he took his time, undoing the slip of a dress—finding not sky-hooks but inbuilt cups inside the top—looking at Meg's body as the black silk pooled around her feet, drinking in its beauty.

But eyes were not enough and soon his hands

skimmed her shape, shoulders, breasts, waist, hips and down her thighs—learning Meg again.

'Your turn,' she whispered huskily, and reached out to undo the buttons on his shirt, her fingers shaking so much they fumbled. A small part of his brain wished he'd listened to why she wouldn't marry him, for surely this was heaven—Meg naked but for a tiny thong, undressing him with shaking hands.

'I might need help.'

She was fumbling with his belt buckle—having trouble because he was shaking, too. Could such restraint be good? He didn't know but couldn't hurry, needing this coming together to be special, but he helped her fingers with the belt and guided them next to the zip, where surely she could feel his erection straining to be free.

Was that a blowfly in the room?

Meg's hands stilled, his trousers now at hip level, but she was fumbling in his pocket now.

'Your pager—is it in your pocket or on your belt?'

No blowfly!

Sam grabbed his trousers and hauled them

up, found his pager in the other pocket and dragged it out.

'Hospital,' he said, and moved towards the phone.

'I'll come with you.' Meg's reaction was instantaneous. She was pulling up her dress, holding it across her breasts.

'Not in that dress, you won't!' Sam told her, and she flashed a smile towards him as she hurried out of the room.

'Pick me up outside.'

She was back in jeans and T-shirt by the time he got the car out. No bra—he'd have to talk to her about that. Bad enough that other men might see her peaking nipples, but worse was that they stirred his body in a manner most inappropriate for a man at work.

'We're not going to the hospital?' she queried as he continued along the Esplanade.

'Wharf area,' he said briefly. 'One of those big trimarans on a dinner cruise has hit something in the bay. Reports are garbled but presumably it was a smaller craft so there could be any number of people in the water.'

'Who's there?'

'Coastguard are on site. They've got some volunteer vessels—probably fishermen who were in the area—bringing people back to the wharf, where the ambulances and some hospital staff are waiting. A trawler's standing by to take us and a couple of experienced divers out. It's carrying extra lights to illuminate the area.'

'Divers? The boat's gone down? Both boats?'

'It sounds that way,' Sam said, but they were already turning into the marine precinct and bright lights shone on a scene of chaos. Light glinted off paramedic overalls and washed across gurneys on which wet, pale patients lay. Meg picked out three nurses she knew, a handful of SES volunteers and Pete and Kristianne as well.

'Don't even look at what's happening there,' Sam warned her as he stopped the car well out of anyone's way and got out, hustling her away from the lights to where a trawler, engine growling impatiently, was waiting by the dock further along.

The smell of fish and salt-encrusted nets

wrapped around Meg as she boarded the vessel, feeling a change in the throb of the engines the moment she was on board. They were off.

'We've lights rigged up on our mast,' the deckhand was explaining to Sam as he showed them where to sit, explaining the accident had happened in the widest part of the bay, fifteen minutes out from shore.

Inside the cabin Meg could see two divers pulling on their wetsuits, zipping up so all in black they looked less like men and more like travellers from a distant planet. The boat's radio was crackling with directions, the skipper's replies inaudible over the thump and grumble of the engines, then as they drew close they saw the lights—and the flotilla of small boats now gathered around the coast-guard vessel.

'The Stingray and the big cruiser VMO 260 can both stay—you'll be useful to carry people back to shore—but the rest of you boats clear the area.'

The order came clearly across the water—someone on the coastguard boat using a mega-phone.

Nothing happened and the loud, mechanical sounding voice spoke again.

'We'll have the police here any minute and any of you still here, aside from those two, will be arrested.'

Meg doubted the water police could arrest all the people on upwards of seven boats, but the threat seemed to have some force as small motors started up and the little boats, most with one or two people in them, eased away—though only far enough to allow space around the accident site. They may not have caught many fish that evening but they'd go home big with news.

The big trawler came alongside the coastguard vessel, and the two divers, then Meg and Sam, were transferred. The deckhand passed across some lightweight stretchers—ones from SES equipment, Meg guessed—and some first-aid packs as well, one of the coastguard crew taking charge of them, everyone working quietly and efficiently. The trawler was then sent to the other side of where the vessels had gone down, to send light towards the sunken boats.

Meg shuddered at the ghostly white bows of

the big trimaran poking up from the bottom of the bay, but there were injured people on the deck in front of her, and work came before pity.

'We're putting them into the recovery position, checking airways and major bleeding, but we've not had time to do much else,' the coastguard man who'd collected the new gear explained. 'There are a couple of bad-looking ones up front—if one of you's a doctor, you might start there.'

Sam picked up one of the packs and followed him, while Meg knelt beside a woman who was lying silently on the deck, on her side but barely breathing.

'Can you hear me? Can you talk?'

Eyelids lifted to reveal grey eyes but they couldn't focus and the woman's eyelids closed again almost immediately. Meg pressed a hand against the woman's chest and felt the faintest movement as she breathed. Ten seconds, feel for ten seconds—the rate was fast but her breathing shallow. Meg felt for expired air next, then reached for oxygen. Air was getting in and out—straight oxygen would help.

Meg spoke to her again and the woman

coughed—gag reflex OK. A nasopharyngeal tube would carry the oxygen directly into her lungs.

Hands moving almost without direction, Meg got the oxygen flowing then felt for the woman's pulse.

Racing—over one hundred beats a minute. Together with the rapid breathing it suggested pneumothorax, a condition where air was getting into the pleural space between the chest wall and the lungs but getting trapped there, unable to get out. As it built up it would not only put pressure on the lungs but on the heart and major blood vessels running through the thoracic cavity.

Meg's mind pictured the accident. Two boats colliding. There'd have been a jar, knocking those who were standing off their feet, those sitting off their chairs—against the table?

She pressed gently against the woman's chest, feeling the distortion of the rib cage at the same time the woman gasped and flinched away from her.

Cracked ribs, possibility of one puncturing a lung, definite possibility of a pneumothorax—

but tension, which could be deadly, or a simple one that could be handled later?

The first two signs of tension pneumothorax, rapid breathing and rapid pulse, were there, and the woman's skin was clammy, but whether from her dunking or shock, Meg couldn't tell.

Very gently Meg turned the woman on her back, unwrapping the blanket that had been tucked around her, needing to examine her for more signs, hearing through a stethoscope the loud sounds on the left side of her chest, seeing distended neck veins as affected vessels battled to get blood through what was like a road-block in their way. And the final clue, the woman's trachea deviating to the right—away from the affected side.

Tension pneumothorax. She needed to release the trapped air by needle thoracentesis—plunging a cannula through the second intercostal space and attaching a syringe so the air could escape.

Meg found the equipment she needed, stripped back the woman's clothing, measured the midclavicular line where the cannula should go and plunged it in. The satisfying hiss of air told her she'd done the right thing, and a movement from the woman suggested she was already feeling better.

IV access next—internal injuries could be causing blood loss and fluid replacement was essential. It was second nature to her now—years of training and practice coming together so she had the woman hooked up to fluid and was contemplating inserting a chest drain to remove the remaining air from the chest cavity when Sam squatted at her side.

'All OK?'

'Apart from the fact my legs are getting too old for this kind of crouching,' Meg told him, 'everything's fine.'

She explained what she'd done, asked about his patients—both now transferred back to shore and left him to insert a chest drain with a one-way valve, while she moved on to the next patient.

A man more concerned about whether his wife had got out safely than his obviously broken leg. Meg checked him out but found no other damage, organised oxygen, fluid, pain relief, splinted the leg, eased him onto a stretcher and tagged him to be taken to shore.

'I can't go without her,' he protested, as two of the coastguard appeared to carry him across to one of the boats doing the shore run.

'She might already have gone ashore. I did hear they had thirty people at the wharf, mostly unharmed. You can't help her here and you're taking up space we need as more people are brought up from the boats.'

'But if they're being brought up, they'll be dead. They'll have drowned. We were celebrating our wedding anniversary.'

He began to cry, and though Meg wished with all her heart she could spare some time to comfort him, he had to go. But what comfort could she offer when the thought of people trapped and drowned filled her with such agonising sorrow herself?

But as the two men lifted the stretcher she heard one say, 'She could be all right. One diver's been up. There's an air pocket there so there's air to breathe.'

And though Meg felt relief, another question soon quelled it.

How long would the air last?

How many people would it sustain?

CHAPTER EIGHT

MORE VICTIMS were brought onto the coastguard vessel, blankets quickly wrapped around them then they were passed along for her or Sam to check.

The divers had first offered oxygen from their own tanks to those trapped below, then had taken tanks down for the victims to share until they could be helped out. Some with the confidence a few gulps of oxygen had given them had even made their own way up to the surface, where willing hands had hauled them aboard.

'I'm going down, there's someone trapped.'

Meg turned from a woman she was tending—bandaging a badly scraped shin—to see Sam struggling into a wetsuit much too small for him.

'It's a man in the galley of the trimaran. I might have to amputate his foot to get him out. You're OK here?'

Meg looked in horror at Sam. He was going down into the dark waters of the bay to cut off someone's foot, and he made it sound…normal?

Or was he speaking that way not to panic her?

She reached out and touched his leg—well, the cold, clammy rubber of the wetsuit on his leg—and said, 'Take care,' hoping her voice didn't quaver enough to give away her horror.

He bent and pressed a hand against her hair.

'I will,' he said, and it sounded like a promise.

But was it a promise he could keep? If the man was trapped, whatever was trapping him could fall on Sam. Trap him! And who would cut *him* free?

She worked on, hoping to escape the thoughts chasing through her head, but although she worked efficiently and spoke cheerfully to all the patients as she tended them, her heart was with Sam while her mind made little bargains with uncaring fate—promising her soul for his safe return.

At last the final passenger had been shipped back to shore—or last but one. Sam and the two divers were still down below, still trying to rescue the trapped man.

How badly was he hurt? Would shock and lack of treatment kill him before they got him out?

Meg walked into the cabin of the coastguard cabin where the captain was talking to someone on his radio.

'How bad are things back on shore?' she asked, as he turned it off and acknowledged her with a nod and an offer of coffee.

She answered with a nod herself, and followed him to a table with an urn on it. A litter of dirty cups and teaspoons showed coffee had been much in demand all evening.

'The most badly injured have been taken straight through to the city,' he told her. 'The Bay hospital has been treating people for shock, keeping a few for observation but on the whole sending home those people who have family or friends to watch over them.'

'How many were there? Did they all survive?'

The man made her coffee then waved his hand towards sugar in a paper bag and milk in its carton.

'We have two fatalities,' he said quietly. 'I'm thinking they were in the speedboat that hit the trimaran. Teenagers, both of them. They were the first taken ashore—one of our blokes went with them on a trawler that was coming in from netting the shallow banks.'

'Did you know them?' Meg asked gently, hoping the pain in his voice was for a different reason. He turned away but not before she saw him swallow hard.

'One young bloke's a neighbour,' he said. 'His mother's had a rough time as it is. Her husband left her a couple of years ago—just took off without a thought for how she'd cope with four young kids. We've all helped out but Josh—the one who died—he… I guess he resented his dad leaving him like that and he's taken it out on the whole world. Angry—that's how he was, all the time. He'd have been speeding across the water, probably with no lights. All that anger…'

Meg hadn't thought her heart could ache so much for someone else, but right now it was aching for Josh's mother.

As much as it had ached for Lucy.

And suddenly she was fiercely glad she'd told Sam she wouldn't marry him. Marriage was too hard. There were too many stresses and strains and bad stuff that could happen—too many heartaches waiting to strike when you least expected them.

Sam! Was Sam all right?

She sipped her coffee and went back to worrying, although her chest still throbbed with the referred pain of a woman she didn't know.

Sam breathed in and out, checking from time to time the dial that showed how much oxygen he had left in his tank.

The two divers were working with pinch bars to try to prise the refrigerated cold room off the man's foot, but the weightlessness of water meant they couldn't get the leverage they needed, and steel plating used in the decking of the trimaran meant they couldn't bash away the deck to free him that way.

Sam held the oxygen mask to the man's nose and supported him, but he guessed there was injury to the foot already, for the man's pallor suggested he was losing blood, though the shadowy water didn't show it.

Unable to communicate apart from basic hand

signals, he had no idea of knowing if the divers'
work was meeting with success. He hoped so—
the idea of amputating the man's foot in such circumstances was making him feel physically ill.
Although in his head he was rehearsing it. The
first thing the divers had done had been cut away
the man's slip-on shoe, thinking to pull his foot
out of it, but the foot wouldn't move.

The ankle was clear, which was good, and he
thought the tarsal bones, the ones closest to the
ankle, could probably be saved. But with the
metatarsals and the phalanges trapped by such a
weight, the chances were they were crushed and
worthless anyway.

But cutting through? Getting through the bones.
No, around the bones—cut through the sinews
and ligaments of the joints but keep as much skin
as possible so the wound can be closed over neatly.

Would half a foot ever be neat?

No, think positive. The man had already been
given a sedating injection—just enough to relax
him—and Sam had put a nerve block in his leg
so he was feeling nothing below the knee.
Everything was ready—should it be necessary.

Pray it would not be!

The divers straightened and gave the signal he'd been dreading. No can do!

OK, it was up to him. Up to him, and speed was essential. Hard to bandage a cut-off foot underwater!

He signalled to the divers to hold the patient and slid lower in the water, first securing a ligature around the man's leg, just above the ankle, hoping it would stop enough blood flow to save the man bleeding to death while he operated. Then with concentrated effort he un- sheathed the first of the scalpels he'd tucked into his weight-belt and more by feel than from the feeble light penetrating the churned-up water, he began to cut, starting right against the steel con- tainer that pressed against the foot, delving deeper as he felt each bone, using his hands to find the joints before pressing hard between them, remembering as he pressed just how tough nerves and sinews and ligaments were.

It was taking for ever.

The man would surely die.

He was running out of oxygen.

They all must be.

Then a movement—an involuntary spasm of the man's calf or thigh muscle—and the foot moved. Sam wrapped a sodden towel around it and held on tightly, signalling to the divers at the same time to take them up.

They rose swiftly, not deep enough to be concerned about the bends, willing hands reaching out to take his patient. Sam tore away his own mask to yell at Meg, whose pale face hung above him.

'Pad and bind his foot then loosen the ligature just slightly, give him oxygen and start fluid IV.'

The man was already gone, and so was Meg. Now all Sam had to do was haul his weary body aboard the vessel and tend his patient.

The twin motors of the coastguard vessel roared as the driver took off, heading back to shore the moment he had Sam and the divers on board.

'He's being well looked after,' one of the crew told Sam as he lifted the oxygen tank from his back, taking its weight while he undid the straps and eased it off his shoulders.

How long had it been since he'd last dived?

He'd certainly been fitter then. His shoulders ached with strain, and getting out of the wetsuit and into his dry trousers and shirt all but exhausted him.

'Hot sweet coffee, mate.'

Another crewman handed him the cup and wrapped a blanket around his shoulders. Just how many blankets did the coastguard carry?

Then, still sipping, he made his way to where Meg had his patient, also blanket-wrapped. The damaged foot was already padded and Meg was tightening the ligature again.

'He's too cold. The crew are heating a fluid bag in their kitchen, but he's shaking with shock and hypothermia.'

'Body heat—it's not for long,' Sam suggested, whipping off his blanket to lie on the deck beside the man. Meg understood and lay down on the other side, cuddling up to the cold, unresponsive body.

But he was breathing, and that, Sam knew, was as good as it would get, until they got him ashore where warming pads in the ambulance would start the process of bringing him back to normal.

Or his temperature back to normal.

Any other normal would be difficult for him for a while.

A crewman approached, a bag of fluid held tentatively aloft. Meg spotted him as well and sprang up.

'You lie here,' she told the crewman, taking the fluid, feeling the temperature of it against her cheek and reaching for the bag already hooked up to the IV access.

She double-checked the label then switched bags. Another crewman came with more blankets.

'Put these on the bilge pump—they mightn't be clean but they're warm. And I haven't been in the water, so my body's warmer than yours.'

He took Sam's place beside the man, while Meg spread the blankets over their patient, tucking them tight across all three of them to trap the two men's body heat around their patient.

The motors revved then stopped. They were back at the wharf. Sam sat back and let the ambulance attendants who scrambled on board shift the man onto a stretcher, then carry him away.

'I'll go with them—you take my car home,' he

said to Meg, whose T-shirt was wet and stained with blood and grease.

'No, you go with him but I'll follow,' she said, taking the keys. 'Whatever staff's on duty will need to be relieved—there'll be work for both of us.'

Sam was too tired to argue—too tired even to think about where they'd been when all of this had begun, but he saw the strain in Meg's white face and the bluish shadows beneath her eyes and though he wanted to argue—to order her home to bed—he knew he wouldn't.

She wouldn't be Meg if she didn't insist on being at the hospital.

'How are you feeling? Up to an hour or so in Theatre?'

Meg was settling the woman with the collapsed lung into a single room where she could be monitored when Sam came through the door.

'The man with the foot?'

Sam nodded.

'I can't send him anywhere until he's stable, and that won't happen until we've done something with his foot. I've got him in Theatre. Kristianne will assist but I'll need a couple of nurses.'

'I'll come, and I'll grab someone else with theatre experience off a ward. I don't particularly want to call in any off-duty staff as we'll be just as busy tomorrow with the patients we've kept here.'

The man's body had been gradually warmed back to within acceptable limits, but he was shocked and had fluid in his lungs—not an ideal patient for surgery, but until the blood vessels in his foot were tied off, he was in danger of haemorrhaging to death.

Meg was glad to see Andy, their most experienced anaesthetist, already in Theatre, watching over the man, checking his sedation, keeping an eye on his breathing and heart rate while Sam and Kristianne worked on his foot.

'We've got to make sure the sutures will hold,' Sam was telling Kristianne, as one by one they tied off bleeding vessels, cauterising the smaller ones so the smell of burning hung in the air. The theatre was quiet, apart from the clatter of instruments and the demands of the two surgeons.

'If we can reattach this strand of muscle to one

of these small bones, it might give him some movement later,' Sam added. 'Enough to make prosthetic toes work.'

The pair worked swiftly, Meg enjoying the rhythm of theatre work as she slapped instruments into waiting hands and dropped soiled swabs into the bin.

Finally, Sam tucked the skin he'd managed to save around the man's truncated foot and sewed it neatly, leaving Kristianne and Meg to dress it.

'Your car keys are in my jeans pocket in the changing room,' Meg called after him, thinking he might now—it was four in the morning—be going home.

He turned back and shook his head.

'You take the car. I'm staying.'

As he walked away, Meg could feel Kristianne's eyes on her and looked up to see questions in them.

'He lives next door—we went to the wharf in his car,' she explained briefly, and the woman's blue eyes brightened perceptibly.

'That's all?' she persisted, as Andrew and an orderly wheeled their patient away.

'Pretty much. He grew up here, so I knew him from before.'

'Hmm!'

'You interested?' Meg had to ask, and Kristianne laughed.

'What woman under a hundred wouldn't be?'

'But you're leaving in a month or so,' Meg protested, aware she was liking this conversation less and less.

'So? I can't have some fun for a month? Actually, it's six weeks. Six weeks with sexy Sam! Has a good ring to it, don't you think?'

Actually, Meg didn't, and she wasn't entirely sure that now she'd turned down Sam's ridiculous proposal he wouldn't take Kristianne up on whatever she might offer.

It was another example of how little they knew of each other.

Just thinking about it made her feel sick! But as soon as she'd helped the other nurse clean up the theatre and had the instruments in the autoclave, she grabbed her grubby clothes and, still in her scrub suit, drove Sam's car home so she could shower and change.

Pride?

She didn't want to think about it, any more than she wanted to think about Kristianne making moves on Sam. She was back within three quarters of an hour, showered and in uniform, and if she was wearing just a touch more make-up than usual, who was to know?

Leaving Sam's car in the car park, she walked through the hospital, starting with the A and E rooms, checking who was still held there, checking staff numbers and who should be sent off duty, who called in to deal with the extra patients.

Doing her job and doing it well—she had been promoted to DON last year—were the things that had brought her satisfaction in the last four years, but today a little devil in some dark corner of her mind was prodding her with his pitchfork and asking if it would be enough for ever.

Of course not, but medicine will be, she told him firmly.

'Lips still moving when you read?'

Sam's voice startled her as she bent over the duty roster in the A and E office. She glanced up and saw the gleam in his eyes. Appreciation that she'd changed?

Or something else?

She didn't have to wait long for clarification. A smile made the gleam seem brighter as he asked, 'Did you have a particular storeroom in mind?'

She had to laugh but the excitement that zoomed through her body and sprinted along her nerves wasn't a laughing matter, but she hid her reaction and said calmly, 'There's a nice one in the corridor next to where the crash cart is kept, but I thought you'd put the kibosh on an affair.'

Had she spoken loudly, that Sam looked around to see if anyone had heard?

But when he said, 'It will not be an affair,' in a very firm voice, she realised he'd looked around to protect his words, not hers. 'That discussion is not finished.'

A squawk from the radio suggested it was— an ambulance was calling in to say they had a young woman in labour on board. 'No obstetrician, no regular doctor, no check-ups along the way, thinks she might be about six or seven months. ETA seven minutes,' the driver finished, and Meg reached for the phone, calling the consultant obstetrician and checking she had a midwife on duty in the labour ward, warning staff there of the new arrival.

'Do you handle most local births?' Sam asked.

'Nearly all of them,' Meg told him. 'Some young women who haven't lived here long might go home to where they grew up to have their first baby, but after that—and with all the locals—they come here. We've good staff, and fathers can live in if the wife needs to stay for more than one night. We've a good home follow-up routine going as well, hospital staff doing home visits for the first three months.'

The patient was little more than a girl—undernourished and grubby-looking—with, to Meg's horror, needle tracks and keloid scarring from needles up both arms.

She was also totally spaced out.

'Was anyone with her? Who called you guys?' Meg asked the attendant who wheeled her in.

'We got a triple zero call from a mobile phone that's got a number block on it, and she was alone when we got there. She was in that old guest house building at the southern end of the Esplanade—the one the developers are pulling down shortly to build the big hotel.'

Meg knew the building and knew it was used as a squat for young people drifting into the Bay, finding life on the streets more comfortable in a place that was both warm and had any number of derelict buildings.

'And a ready supply of drugs apparently!' Meg muttered to herself as Sam followed the patient into the trauma room.

Sam was talking gently to her, asking how far apart the contractions were.

She lifted her thin wrist to show she wasn't wearing a watch and shook her head. Meg nodded to the nurse to start timing them and asked her to strap a foetal heart monitor around the girl's belly. Then, while Sam talked on, inserting a catheter and taking blood for testing, Meg began to take note of the young woman's status.

'Everything up,' she was able to tell Matt when he arrived. 'Pulse 110 beats a minute, respirations 22 a minute, temperature 99.8, blood pressure 140 over 95. The foetal heart rate is good—158 beats a minute—and she's having contractions…'

Meg looked across at the nurse.

'Seven minutes between them.'

'Do you know when the baby is supposed to be due?' Matt asked, his voice so gentle Meg knew why women loved him as a doctor.

'I think at Christmas. Or some time then,' the young woman said. 'But if it comes now, it'll die, won't it?'

'Not necessarily,' Matt told her, while the medical staff in the room all mentally computed the woman must be about thirty weeks pregnant.

'Better it dies,' the woman said. 'It'll be all screwed up with drug addiction. Not much chance for the poor little thing.'

Meg stared at the young woman, at the good bones in her face that showed she had been pretty before drugs and disease had taken their toll.

'There's no such thing as no chance,' she protested, while Matt explained he was going to give her something that might stop the pre-term labour.

'The longer you can go in your pregnancy, the more chance the baby will have of survival.'

'But I don't want the baby!' the girl, Melody, protested. 'Who'll look after it?'

Matt, ignoring her protests, was hooking up a drip to the cannula the ambos had inserted in her arm.

'You need fluid anyway, and maybe some methadone. Have you been on a programme?'

Melody nodded.

'Got hooked on that just as easy, and with the fuss you have to go through to get it, might just as well stick to H.'

'Do you want to get off it? Want us to help you?'

Sam spoke so gently tears filled the girl's eyes.

'It's no use,' she said. 'My mum tried to help, and if she couldn't do it, why should you be able to?'

'We could try,' Meg offered. 'And if you like, we could contact your mum. Maybe she'd like to be with you.'

The tears spilled over then and rolled in steady streams down the emaciated cheeks.

'She doesn't know about this,' Melody finally managed, but the careful way she cupped her hand around her swollen belly and rubbed it gently suggested she wasn't nearly as uncaring about this unborn babe as her tough talk had suggested.

Sam wheedled her mum's phone number out of her and left the cubicle, while Meg waited until Matt had finished his examination then arranged for Melody to be shifted to a single room.

'I think she's had a shot recently—you might have trouble as she's coming off,' Matt told Meg as the girl was wheeled away.

'We've handled it before. We'll manage,' Meg said, sure that if Sam had had A and E experience in a big Sydney hospital he'd know even more than they did about heroin addiction and how to handle it in a hospitalised patient.

'Her mum's in Brisbane. She'll drive up and, giving her time to pack and get the cat to the cattery, she should be here in about six hours.'

'Mum sounds like a very efficient woman,' Meg said, smiling at Sam because she was relieved Melody would have family support— and also because he was Sam!

She asked him about his experience with drug-addicted patients, explaining they'd had a doctor at the hospital who knew a lot but he'd gone back to England, and since then they'd gone on text-books and help from the drugs hotline in Brisbane.

'I've seen more of it than I would have thought possible,' Sam said, his face looking tired and drawn. The memory of kids he hadn't been able to help or the result of a night without sleep? Or both? 'I'll keep a special eye on her.'

Meg told him where Melody was and returned to the rosters she'd been checking. It was nearly change of shift for those working a split shift and she still had no idea what nursing staff members were on duty or how many she might need for the rest of the day.

By five o'clock the hospital had settled down. The man with the amputated foot had been trans-ferred to Brisbane as he came from there and had family support, as well as specialists who could help his rehabilitation.

Melody's mother had arrived so Melody was now clean and clad in a beautiful silk nightdress while the tocolytic drug—to prevent the prema-ture labour—seemed to be working. She couldn't be said to be stable but she was talking more positively about kicking her habit and was responding to the drug regime recommended by addiction specialists Sam had contacted in Sydney.

So when the man in question poked his head into the office and said, 'Come on, let's go home,' Meg didn't argue, although she knew the 'going home' thing would be taken literally. They were both too tired to think of anything but sleep.

'We'll catch up,' Sam said, as if he'd read her mind. He slung an arm around her shoulder and guided her out of the hospital towards the car park.

'Will we?' she said, too tired to stop her thoughts becoming words, worrying that the more physical contact she had with Sam—more physical pleasure and delight—the harder it would be to keep saying no.

Though he mightn't ask her again...

'Of course. For a start, there's a whole conversation of yours I must have missed, looking at the way your hair fell, and your eyes sparkled in the moonlight. I'm not taking your no for an answer without hearing the reason.'

So what was the reason?

It was to do with love. Not her love for she *did*

love him, and she was pretty sure it was the grown-up Sam she loved and not a hangover from the past.

More to do with Sam and love…

And telling him she loved him would give him too much power—way too much—on top of all he already had with his ability to make her bones go weak and her nerves tingle whenever he was in her vicinity.

She climbed into the car and asked if he'd put down the top then drive the long way home so the wind could blow in her hair all the way along the Esplanade.

CHAPTER NINE

'I was going to drive this way anyway,' Sam said, as they turned onto the southern end of the Esplanade. 'Can you show me the building where Melody was squatting?'

So much for romantic, wind-in-the-hair type drives!

'Next block,' she told him. 'It used to be called Sea-Spray when it was a guest house, and I think the developers are keeping the name for the new building when it goes up. There!'

She pointed at the chunky, art deco style building on a rise that gave it views across the bay.

Sam slowed the car.

'Do you think many people use it as a squat?'

Meg sighed, more helplessness than tiredness in the soft sound.

'I suppose so,' she said. 'It looks solid and is

probably dry and the Bay has its own share of runaways as well as people who drift in.'

'Are there shelters? Places they can get a bed, go for a meal?'

'Not as such.' He eased the car back onto the road as Meg explained. 'The problem's fairly recent. I mean, for years the Bay has been seen as somewhere to retire, a place where oldies go. It didn't exactly ring bells for generation X or Y or whatever they're up to now with alphabetical generations. But since the island became world heritage listed and the whale-watching boats started taking tourists out to see the whales, backpackers' hostels have been set up to accommodate young people from all over the world. I guess it was inevitable other young people would follow.'

'But because it's a recent phenomenon it doesn't mean someone shouldn't be helping,' Sam protested, turning onto their stretch of the wide road that followed the winding shoreline.

'People are helping. There's a church group takes a coffee van out on the streets late at night—late here being about ten o'clock—and offers to find accommodation for people who have nowhere to go. That's not ideal because during the whale-watching season there's virtually no accommodation, and as that coincides with winter down south, we have more drifters than usual here at that time.'

'So,' Sam said as he pulled up outside the cottage, 'we need more accommodation for old people with no money and some accommodation for young people with nowhere to go. Probably a multi-faceted drug programme as well...'

Meg turned and stared at him.

'What's this? One man's campaign to save the Bay?'

Sam didn't answer, but she saw the determination in his face.

Had he hurt his mother so badly he was going to dedicate the rest of his life to making up for it?

He didn't answer, though he turned to look at her and touched his fingertips to her cheek.

'I'm too pooped to get out and open the car door for you, so forgive my manners and go get some sleep.'

The end bit had sounded like a gentle order, but the rest? Something had changed between them. Because she'd asked too many questions?

But had she?

She heard the quiet engine move the car forward to his place as she walked towards her cottage.

The answer to *that* question was easy. She hadn't asked nearly as many as she wanted to ask—would ask if she got the chance. That was the whole point of saying no to his proposal—well, that and her own plans—but they really didn't know each other and how else to get to know than through questions?

If they were answered...

So many things were rattling around in Meg's mind she doubted sleep would come, but she'd no sooner closed her eyes than oblivion took her, or so it seemed when she woke at midnight, hungry and disoriented. Pulling on her robe, she stumbled into the kitchen, where the cat was sitting on the bench, looking out the window. His water bowl still had water in it, but his dry food bowl was empty. She opened a tin of salmon she bought very occasionally as a special treat for both of them, spread half of it on toast for herself and gave the other half to him.

'I know in some intrinsic way I love him,' she said to the cat, who, now fed, deigned to wind around her calves. 'Could he feel the same about me, but be covering it up behind the bland practicality of statements like "I think we should get married"?'

Meg didn't know, but she did know marrying without love would be accepting second best— like being a nurse when what she really, really wanted was to be a doctor. It wasn't that nursing wasn't a wonderful profession or that she didn't find it deeply satisfying, it just wasn't *her* dream.

Any more than marrying without love—the heady, intoxicating, to-hell-with-the-rest-of-the-world feeling she had experienced just once before—would be right for her.

Not again.

She explained all this to the cat, who had taken up his post on the bench again, keeping watch for night intruders in her back yard, then went back to bed. But this time sleep didn't come, and in the end she got up, pulled on an old swimsuit, grabbed a towel and went down to the beach.

Midnight swims had been daring, sneaky adventures when she'd been young, but now she often took to the water after dark, knowing the exercise would tire her out. She kept to the shallows for safety's sake.

Sam was waiting on the beach when she came out, water streaming from her exhausted body.

'I thought from all the splashing it was you. Long, clean swimming strokes, Megan, and try not to break the water with your kick.'

She stared at him.

'Were you swimming when I came down?' she demanded. 'I didn't see you.'

'I swam out, not along the shoreline.'

'Swimming out is stupid—especially at night when there's no one around. What if you got a cramp?'

'Would anyone care—even notice—if I didn't come back from a swim?'

'Oh, for heaven's sake, what's this? Self-pity, Sam? Asking for a little comfort? For an assurance that your life matters? Or are you being seventeen again, taking risks for the thrill of it?'

Meg snatched up her towel from where it lay beside him and stepped away to shake the sand out of it before wrapping it around her shoulders as the night air made her shiver.

'Or to hurt your mother?'

The answer struck her so suddenly she could only whisper it as she sat down on the sand beside him.

'That's why you did it, isn't it? Back then?'

'It's only since I came back that I've put it all together,' he said quietly. 'It was one last swim—one last penance if you like—but, Megan, when I think—'

'You were hurting, Sam, and you hit back. Not admirable perhaps but at seventeen understandable. But what's changed? What did you find out about your father that kissing me is now OK?'

He didn't answer for so long Meg counted forty tiny waves whisper up the beach then shush back into nothingness.

'I had to go through Mum's papers after her death, looking for insurance policies, bank accounts, all the things you need to do. She had a bundle of letters in an old chocolate box. Tied with a blue ribbon. How corny can you get? Letters from Daryl Westwood.'

He paused as if Meg should know the name but although she might have heard of a family called Westwood, the Daryl part wasn't ringing any bells.

'You didn't go to the Bay High School, which is why the name means nothing. To me it meant local hero! He was school captain in his final year, captain of the cricket and rugby teams, best debater, top of his class and all-round good guy from all accounts, although history does build up its heroes.'

'So?' Meg probed when she'd counted another forty waves.

'His photo was up on the wall in our assembly hall, and every kid who went to Bay knew the story—knew how he'd finished school and was going on to university in Brisbane to do medicine. His parents and younger sister were all driving down with him to see him settled into college when they slammed into a semitrailer and were killed—the whole family wiped out.'

Meg reached out and took Sam's hand, squeezing his fingers tightly.

Another forty—maybe fifty—waves washed up the beach.

'In case I hadn't heard the stories, the newspaper cuttings of the accident, all brown and brittle, cracking at the folds, were in the box. The letters made it clear the affair was a secret—apparently Westwoods weren't supposed to associate with the daughters of Italian cane farmers. Maybe Mum's parents had forbidden it as well. But the last letter had a train ticket to Brisbane in it, and a form already filled out by Daryl for Mum to complete—a declaration of an intention to get married.'

Meg felt tears for Gina sliding down her cheeks, and her chest felt so heavy she leant against Sam's shoulder, then rational thought subsumed the emotion.

'But if he was dead couldn't Gina have told you your father had died? He was this great fellow but he died?'

She felt Sam's chest move as he took in a deep breath.

'Yes, she could have, but the way I figure it, I'd

just have asked more questions. His name, for one thing.'

He moved and turned towards her so he could look into her eyes.

'This guy was looked on as a hero, Meg. Mourned by the whole town as a golden youth of tremendous promise cut off in his prime. Do you think the town would have accepted Mum's word that he was the father of her baby? Do you think Mum would have wanted, even with the proof she had, to somehow dishonour his memory in this way? Had his parents survived, or if he'd had other relatives, maybe she would have told them, if only so they knew something of him had lived on, but Mum was Mum, good at keeping her own counsel—even to the stage of letting it drive a wedge between us.'

He sounded so exhausted Meg put her arm around his shoulder.

'Have you slept at all?' she asked.

'Like a log until midnight, when my biological clock suggested it was time to get up and have some breakfast.'

'One night without sleep and body clocks go

wrong,' Meg agreed, mainly because she didn't know what else to say.

They sat in silence until the sky began to lighten in the east, and the moonlight lost its brilliance, then as the first blush of pink heralded another dawn, Sam turned and kissed her, wrapping his arms around her and drawing her close.

Damp, sticky from the salt water and sandy from sitting on the beach—it wasn't an ideal way to take that kiss further, and as if by mutual consent they stood up, linked arms behind each other's backs and walked up the path to the road.

'My place!' Sam said, and Meg didn't argue. After all, it was still her place in her head. They showered together, touching, loving with their touches, but keeping the best of their excitement for the bed. Eventually, twined together, they finally found sleep again, Meg nestled close against Sam's chest, his arm heavy across her body.

She'd come home…

'We're late for work.'

Sam looked down into the face of the woman

in his arms, seeing sleep creases on her cheeks and shy wonder in her eyes.

'I hate that,' she told him, but she didn't move, snuggled against him like a pup against its mother, so close she might be trying to climb inside his skin.

'Now can we get married?'

He knew it was the wrong thing to say as soon as the words escaped his lips, but he'd been feeling so content—even happy—with Meg entangled in his arms.

Not any more! She was sitting up and frowning at him, a look of disbelief on her face. Then she wiped away the frown with an impatient swipe of her hand and spoke.

'OK, your mother getting pregnant out of wedlock might be an excuse for you to keep harping on this marriage thing every time we have sex, but I've already said no, Sam. We're grown-ups now, we can take precautions against pregnancy. In fact, although you haven't asked, I'm already on the Pill. Have been since I had Lucy because it helps regulate things for me. But there's more to marriage than sex and it's time you realised that. Do you have a robe I can put on to go home?'

She was out of bed, delving in his wardrobe now—in the hanging part, not the drawers where she might see her underwear and start to wonder about fetishes as well as the other suspicions she obviously harboured about him.

'You can't go home in a robe,' he protested, as she pulled on his old navy towelling robe and tied the belt around her slim waist. That wasn't what he'd wanted to say, of course. What he'd wanted to say was, *Why won't you marry me?* But he knew it would sound whiny and she'd already accused him of self-pity once today.

Although self-pity had been the furthest thing from his head, he'd been stating what he saw as a fact. No relations—no one to mourn him.

Though Meg would.

He knew that now.

So why—?

But she was gone, obviously thinking his objection to her robe-wearing departure from his house unworthy of comment.

He climbed out of bed, showered and dressed,

then considered phoning his psychiatrist ex-girlfriend, not for counselling but for some advice on the female of the species.

His lack of understanding of the way they thought had to be at the root of his lack of success with long-term relationships. He'd always known they were different—would *he* have gone to Sydney with his mother if she'd behaved as badly towards him as he had towards her? Most definitely not, but his mother, and women in general, he'd deduced, had an infinite capacity for love—providing it through even the most difficult of circumstances.

And for all she said they didn't know each other. He knew Meg loved him—knew it in his bones, the way he knew his blood was flowing through his veins although he couldn't feel, or hear, or see it.

She wasn't in her office when he arrived at work, though when he did his round, signs she'd been ahead of him were everywhere. The nursing staff, he'd noticed before, moved more quickly and spoke more cheerfully when Meg was about, not because she was a martinet—or not that he had seen—but because she had the power to enthuse her staff with her own commitment and determination.

He caught up with her in Melody's room. It was bright with flowers, but they only served to make the wan girl in the bed look even paler.

'I can't do it,' she said. 'It hurts too much.'

Sam said good morning, eyed the drip and picked up her chart. Had the contractions started again?

'But you want to do it,' Meg said. 'For your own sake. Forget about the baby and your mother, it's for you that you want to kick the habit. So you can get your life back again. You're young, you're bright and, yes, it will be terribly hard, but what's the alternative? Being dead before you're twenty? Having nothing but an occasional rosy haze when you've got drugs, and sleazy desperation when you need more?'

'You'd have persuaded me off it,' Sam offered, 'but my guess is Melody's in too much pain to even think about it. So, let's see what we can safely do to make you feel better, Melody.'

He didn't mention the 'without harming the baby' that was ringing in his head. Right now, the baby was the last thing on Melody's mind. He checked the notes he had from the specialist at the Sydney centre and asked Meg to fetch what he needed—a cocktail of drugs that would ease her into sleep, blanketing the need that was grinding her nerves to pieces.

He was feeding this into the drip, Meg having departed, when a woman who was obviously Melody's mum came bustling in with more flowers.

'You're not giving her drugs, I hope,' she said to Sam. 'Cold turkey—isn't that what they call it? And isn't this the best place to do it, right here in hospital where she can be watched?'

'And strapped to the mattress if necessary, with her body writhing in agony?'

Mrs Carter gave him a dirty look, but Sam guessed she was hurting every bit as much as her daughter, and as Melody drifted off to sleep, he took the mother's hand and sat her in one of the visitor chairs, sitting down on the other one himself.

'There's nothing to be gained by giving her more pain than she needs to suffer. We've stopped the labour for the moment, but what we really need to do, for the sake of the baby, is to keep her here so we can monitor her. Not for the ten weeks until the baby's due, but long enough to build her up and help her towards at least a partially drug-free life. Not everyone can get off heroin—or if they do and get onto methadone, they often can't get off that. But at least we have a chance to help Melody through the worst of withdrawal, and in doing that we're giving the baby a chance.'

The woman's tired blue eyes looked into his.

'What about the baby?' she asked. 'Won't it be addicted? And she hasn't been eating properly—you can see that. What about the baby?'

'The baby's likely to be small, and within a few days develop signs of narcotic withdrawal. It is potentially fatal but if we can do a switch to methadone while Melody's in hospital there's a lot better chance for the baby. The symptoms of narcotic withdrawal are general jitteriness, bad sleep patterns, a wailing cry—very high-pitched—sneezing, sometimes seizures. We'll know and we'll be ready to treat the baby as well.'

'If she stays here,' Mrs Carter said doubtfully.

'It's not that I don't think you're up to it, but if I took her back to Brisbane with me, there'd be more specialists—there are drug referral centres and special hospitals for people on drugs.'

'You must do what you think best, but sometimes in a smaller town you get more support than you would in the city.'

Mrs Carter considered this then shrugged her shoulders.

'I'll have to think about it,' she said, then, as Sam stood up to leave, she touched his arm.

'Stupid, isn't it, how mothers think about their kids? This one's done enough a thousand times to make me hate her, yet somehow it only makes me love her more.'

It so utterly echoed his earlier thoughts about his own mother that he looked up, wondering if she was playing him like a puppet.

But Melody's mother's declaration disturbed him in another way. He'd been thinking women's love was strong enough to withstand anything, while maybe it was mother's love.

Meg was in her office. He went in and shut the door behind him.

'And if I want it open?' she said, looking up, her face unreadable. But this was Meg, the woman who'd cried his name as they'd made love only hours earlier, the woman who'd given all she had to him—opened up her very soul, it had seemed—during their love-making.

'I need to talk to you. Really need to talk. The other night, at the restaurant, you told me why you didn't want to marry me, and I was thinking of your baby, of Lucy, and didn't hear what you said. Will you tell me again?'

'Right here and now?' The frown was easy to read. She didn't think much of the idea.

But he stayed where he was and nodded, watching her hand reach out to pick up a pen, her fingers fiddling with it.

'I've got a plan, you see,' she began. 'A long-term plan. That's why Mum selling the house and having to move into the cottage infuriated me so much. Mum, of course, thinks the plan is stupid because I already have a career and should now be thinking marriage and babies.'

So he'd have an ally in Mrs Anstey!

Meg had stopped twiddling the pen and was

now looking out the window at the gardens surrounding the hospital.

He walked around and squatted in front of her,
rested a hand on her knee.

'Tell me the plan.'

She looked into his eyes, her face serious.

'All I ever wanted to be was a doctor. You know
that. We were both going to do medicine—
practise together. Well, that dream didn't die
when you went out of my life, but it did meet a
hurdle when I got married. I think I told you I'd
done my pre-med degree and first year, then I
was sick carrying Lucy so I deferred second year.
When she was born—when we went to
Melbourne—well, I had to borrow money—a
lot of money—and if I'd gone back to finish my
degree I'd have ended up with even more debts.'

The words were stated in such a matter-of-fact
manner it made the pain Sam could hear beneath
them even harder to bear. His chest constricted,
and though he wanted to say something, there
were no words to help remembered pain.

'The school of nursing offered me credits for
most of my pre-med and first-year subjects, so I

only had to do one more year to get my nursing certificate and most of that I could do part time, working as an aide at the same time.'

'Paying off these debts? What about your husband? Weren't the debts his as well? Or your parents? Your father?'

Pain no longer hidden, Meg's anguished eyes met his.

'I couldn't ask Dad. He was so protective of me, loved me so much,' she whispered. 'I know I disappointed him, not finishing medicine, but he never said a word. He died six months ago—a massive stroke. I didn't even get a chance to say goodbye.'

Sam took her hands and held them tightly. What he really wanted to do was take her in his arms and cradle her, hold her close until all the pain washed away.

But she was strong, his Meg—this new Meg. She sat motionless for a while, regathering her inner resources, then gave a watery smile and continued.

'I think Dad gave away most of the money he made. It used to drive Mum wild. There was always someone in need as far as Dad was concerned, and being paid in carrots or cabbages had always been OK with him. So, no, there was no way I'd have asked him for money. And Charles—well, he hadn't wanted Lucy to go to Melbourne anyway. But I was OK. I knew I could earn good money nursing, and as soon as I'd paid the debt and had enough saved to cover basic living costs for three years, I'd go back and pick up where I'd left off my degree.'

'I was OK,' she'd said? How could anyone who'd lost their child have been OK?

How could anyone then calmly make a plan for the future?

With difficulty, Sam guessed, but she'd also had to do it as a way of putting her life back together—giving her life a focus. That he *could* understand!

But she was smiling again now—a better smile.

'Even with moving into the cottage and having to pay rent, I should reach my financial goal by the end of next year. I'd thought it would be this Christmas, but I've waited this long I can wait another year.'

He shook his head.

'Megan, you're twenty-nine, you'll be thirty-four by the time you finish, then internship. Is this *really* what you want?'

Meg looked at him, perversely thinking his knees must be getting sore, squatting as he was while she poured out her heart to him.

But how to answer?

'Yes, it is, Sam,' she said, because it always had been—because, except in fantasies and day-dreams, Sam had never featured in her future.

He could now.

He'd asked her to marry him.

Twice.

But what Sam was offering wasn't what she wanted from him. She wanted love and she wasn't sure Sam even knew the meaning of the kind of love she sought. Oh, he loved her in his way…

'And because of this—your plan—you won't marry me?'

She answered yes because that was easier than explaining thoughts and feelings she didn't fully understand herself, and saw him wince as he stood up.

'This conversation isn't over,' he said carefully, then he crossed the room, opened the door and walked out, poking his head back in to smile and ask, 'Store cupboard in an hour?'

She had to laugh, although this reminder of Sam's ability to make her laugh underlined her doubts about sticking to 'The Plan'.

He was waiting on his veranda when she arrived home, late as usual but today because she'd stopped to talk to Melody when she'd finished work.

'Come up and have a drink.'

Order or invitation?

Either way, the physical loving they'd shared had desire rampaging through her body, and although she could control it at work—and she hadn't even thought of store cupboards!—now she wanted to be near him, whether ordered or invited.

She parked her car, then glanced down at her uniform.

'Five minutes for a shower?' she suggested.

'I could get you out of that ghastly uniform faster than that!'

Tempting, but she really needed a shower and

showering alone would certainly be quicker than showering with Sam.

'Five minutes,' she told him firmly, and hurried inside the cottage.

The cat was already on Sam's veranda when she arrived, sitting by Sam's chair, accepting homage from his fingers.

'Traitor,' Meg told the cat, and Sam shook his head.

'No way! He's just pre-empting your next move—shifting in with me.'

Her heart leapt. Living with Sam? Talk about dreams and fantasies coming true!

Caution suggested she think it through, so she didn't reply, instead sitting down in one of the low-slung chairs and accepting the glass of cold wine he handed her.

He'd pulled the chairs close together so they sat shoulder to shoulder, and his free hand, cool from holding her glass, came to rest on her knee.

'I have the answer,' he declared, looking not at her but out across the Bay. 'If you really don't mind not starting university again for another year, that would give me time to get the new hospital up and running here, put in good staff, a medical administrator, look at other projects my manager can work on, like accommodation for old people and a shelter of some kind for the young ones, then we'll both go to Brisbane and I'll get a job down there while you study. I could even work part time and do a house-husband thing so you're not stressed out with study and the house stuff.'

Now he looked at her, his face alight with the simplicity of it all, his smile declaring it was a done deal—for why wouldn't she go along with it?

Meg gulped her drink, mentally berating herself for not telling the truth in the first place— but how could she have explained the love thing when she didn't understand it herself?

How to kill his hopes?

She took another gulp of wine and, seeing her glass almost at the empty stage, Sam got up, without the chair entangling him, and went to fetch the bottle.

She waved it away, knowing all the wine in the world wouldn't help.

'The plan was only part of it,' she began, as

Sam sat down again beside her—but didn't put his hand on her knee.

'The rest?'

She turned to him, searching his face, hoping to see a glimmer of understanding though she knew that would be impossible, for what had she given him to understand?

But maybe he did understand, for he took her hand and held it between both of his.

'Is it to do with having children? I could under-stand that, Meg. You lost Lucy and might not want to risk facing that pain again.'

'No, Sam, it's not children. I'd love to have children—three or four—comes of being an only child myself, I guess. I know I'm leaving things late but, no, it's not to do with kids.' This part at least she could answer honestly, and she knew he'd hear the truth in her words.

'It's to do with love,' she finally admitted. 'I can't explain it clearly because it's very mixed-up in my mind, but I married Charles without loving him—not loving him the way I knew I should, with a love that would carry us both through the very toughest times, that would let us fight and yet still love, go through death and yet still love. It wasn't the kind of love that would stand up against the tests life throws at you. The deep-down, in the bones and muscle and sinew kind of love.'

'And you don't feel that kind of love for me?'

Sam spoke so softly Meg barely heard the words, and in a tree across the Esplanade a kookaburra laughed—uproariously.

She knew she should answer the question but answering it honestly would give Sam too much power. He'd take her love and use it as a weapon to push for marriage.

'I don't think *you* feel it, Sam,' she said at last. 'Oh, I know you love me—in the way you've always loved me. Meg the friend, and now Meg the lover. This other love—the love I need—is more than that. But it's the kind of love that takes up so much space it leaves you vulnerable, and that's the one thing you've always hated feeling—the one thing you've always been on guard against.'

He stood up again, filled her glass and walked away, through to the kitchen to put the wine back in the refrigerator, she assumed, and when he returned it was as if the conversation hadn't happened.

'I bought a couple of steaks on the way home. I'll cook you dinner. Veggies or salad with your steak?'

Her heart raced—was that it? Was that all he had to say?

'Salad, thanks,' she managed, damned if he was going to get away with playing cool all on his own. She put down her glass so she wouldn't spill the wine and clambered out of the chair, picking up the glass and following him into the kitchen.

'Can I help?'

He turned and smiled.

'In those shorts you're more of a distraction than a help, but if you want a job, you can pick out what you'd like in a salad in the fridge. I've some pears and soft blue cheese in there some-where—they go well together.'

Sure they did!

Meg forgot the cool, set down her drink so she couldn't throw it at him, folded her arms and let fly.

'That's it? I open up my heart to you and

suddenly we're talking about pears and blue cheese in a salad?'

'Soft blue cheese,' Sam corrected. 'I don't think hard blue goes nearly as well with it. Gorgonzola is the best, but it doesn't seem to find its way to the Bay.'

Meg was sorry she'd put down her drink.

'I don't want to talk about cheese!' she stormed.

'And I don't want to talk about love. Not right now, and definitely not with you all steamed up the way you are. I thought an intelligent woman like you might have figured that out.'

He turned from the stove where he'd set a ridged griddle over a high gas flame.

'I need to think about what you said, Meg. You've obviously been thinking about it, so can't you allow me to do the same? Yes, some of what you said rang bells but not knowing love—or how to love? Harsh judgements, Megan.'

Hurtful judgements, she realised now. Very hurtful.

She moved towards him, putting her arms around him from behind, while he dropped the steaks onto the heated griddle.

'I told you I was muddled,' she whispered. 'I spoke to try to sort my thoughts, not to hurt you.'

He moved within her grasp, holding her in return and bending his head to kiss her on the lips.

'I need to think about it,' he repeated. 'Heaven forbid I should cause you more pain than I've already caused in your life, Megan.'

Another kiss then he walked her backwards across the kitchen to where she'd left her wine.

'Have a drink while I rescue the steaks and nuke a couple of potatoes,' he said, then he smiled. 'You'll need your strength seeing as I took you up on the affair option last night. No need for us to forgo that pleasure!'

Wasn't there?

When every night she spent in Sam's arms would weaken her resolve?

How could she have been so stupid as to have suggested it?

How could she not have known that making love with Sam would mean so much?

CHAPTER TEN

MELODY CARTER went into true labour two days later. The baby girl was tiny but apart from that didn't show any of the signs of prematurity. She gave her first cry spontaneously, breathed for herself with no sign of respiratory distress, had no difficulty feeding or passing urine. And though she was slightly jaundiced, Dr Chan, who examined her at birth, suggested she was closer to full term— maybe thirty-six or thirty-seven weeks gestational age.

Melody was a long way from recovery to her addiction, but she was following the regimen laid out for her, and she admitted she could have been wrong about the date of the baby's conception.

Meg refused to think of all the reasons that could be offered for this confusion, concentrating instead on the girl herself, and the tiny daughter Melody was doubtful about accepting.

Mrs Carter was equally doubtful.

'She sees herself having to bring the baby up if Melody gets back on drugs,' Sam said, coming into the nursery to find Meg cuddling the fretful baby.

Her low birth weight could explain her poor sleeping habits but the paediatrician had warned them it was likely to be foetal alcohol syndrome.

Meg smiled at Sam—not in agreement but because, after a weekend of loving, it had become something she couldn't control. See Sam, smile—easy as that. And it was getting harder to control the other reactions she had to seeing Sam—the pleasurable ache inside her body, the flush of heat remembering brought, the skittering of excitement across her skin.

'You can see her point,' she managed to reply, probably far too late for his smile had broadened. Having an affair with a colleague was proving every bit as difficult as she'd imagined it would be, but though earlier that morning he'd tempted her with the store-cupboard suggestion, they hadn't, as yet, had to resort to it—the nights brought loving enough.

'You getting clucky?'

He nodded to the baby in her arms, and she knew he was thinking her desire for a baby might outweigh what he claimed was her unrealistic attitude to love.

Oh, he'd thought about what she'd said, but argued she was wrong—his love for Meg had held through thirteen years apart—of course it would hold through anything life would throw at them.

Meg studied him as he took the tiny girl—unnamed because of the doubt Melody still felt. He examined her very gently and soothed her fretful cries with his fingertip across her temple.

Yes, she was getting clucky, Meg realised. Almost clucky enough to give up the dream…

But clucky enough to live without the love she needed?

Tough question.

Sam settled the baby in its crib, his arm aching with a need to stretch it around Meg's waist, his body yearning for them to be standing arm in arm by the crib of their own child.

Damn the hospital grapevine. He put his arm around her waist and drew her close.

'I *do* love you,' he murmured, and she turned and flashed the smile that made his heart stand still.

'I know you do,' she acknowledged, and Sam knew they'd moved to another place in their relationship. A place where getting married might be closer.

But it was his insistence on marriage—his talk of it—that seemed to symbolise to Meg all that was wrong in his way of loving.

Puzzling over this, he dropped a quick kiss on her hair, caught the smile on the face of the nurse who walked in at that moment and, uncertain whether to be happy or embarrassed, headed back to his office.

Martin Goodall was coming down the corridor on his way to see Melody, who, in what seemed to be a recurring theme of faulty valves and heart murmurs in Sam's life these days, had been found to have one. And suddenly Sam remembered a scrap of conversation that had bothered him the last time he'd seen Martin.

'As well as working for you, was Mum seeing you for her heart?'

Martin was startled but recovered quickly enough.

'She was. She had a heart murmur. Not bad enough to concern her when she was young but she needed to have regular check-ups.'

Martin bustled away, leaving Sam standing in the corridor.

Heart murmur—leaking valve? Surely he should have known that? Not as a child or teenager, perhaps, but later on—particularly once he'd started studying medicine!

Should she have told him, or should he have asked?

Was this what Meg meant about love not going deep enough?

More confused than ever, he remained where he was, thinking of his mother, of the news he'd heard only three months ago—the news that she'd had heart problems.

Not only heart problems, but a heart so degenerated by the work it had been doing it had been too late for an operation of any kind to save it.

No heroics, his mother had said, but there needn't have been heroics if she'd been treated earlier.

If he'd known…

'Taken root there?' Coralie Stephens came sailing past. 'How's our baby? I guess that's where you've been. Word has it you spend almost as much time in there as Meg does. Maybe the two of you should get together.'

The wink she gave told him the news of their relationship was all around the hospital.

He and Meg should get together?

When his mother had had what had most likely been a congenital heart condition and Meg had had a baby with heart problems.

Meg, who wanted children…

Meg, who had already lost one baby…

His car was in its usual position under the house but there was no sign of Sam when Meg came home, piping hot fish and chips calling to her from their wrapping.

He'd be on the beach. She'd take their dinner down there.

She went into her place to get a huge towel to

spread on the sand, some wet towelettes for their fingers, and a bottle of cold water. Picnic ready, she made her way down to the beach, seeing a solitary swimmer heading back to shore.

He'd swum straight out?

She couldn't swear to it. Maybe he'd swum along the shoreline and had just turned to come back before she saw him.

Would she ask?

She didn't think so. For all their physical closeness there was still constraint hovering just beyond the edges of that togetherness.

'Fish and chips,' she called as he stood up and walked out of the water. He hesitated just slightly, then bent to get his towel, giving his body a perfunctory rub before walking towards where she'd spread the blanket.

'This what you call your turn to cook?' he said, sitting down but not as close as she'd expected.

'You know my limit is tinned salmon on toast, though I can do eggs and bacon at a pinch, and have been known to throw together a good salad.'

He smiled, but not a Sam smile that made her

heart sing little la, la, la notes up and down the scale.

'Fish and chips are great beach food,' he assured her, more Dr Sam than Sam the lover.

'What is it?' she asked, poking a chip into her mouth, though she knew she wouldn't taste its delicious saltiness.

He took her hand, turned it over and pressed a kiss into the palm, carefully folding her fingers over it before he returned it to her lap.

'Eat your fish and chips first,' he ordered.

'First? Eat before you throw some bombshell at me? What are fish and chips supposed to taste like when you've said something like that to me?'

This time he took both her hands.

'I think you're right about what you call the love thing, Megan,' he said, his voice sounding so decisive she knew he meant every word. 'What I feel, for whatever reason, isn't what you need or deserve. No marriage, no affair, but for friendship's sake, and because I love you as a friend, go ahead and make arrangements to start uni in the new year—first semester. I'll fund it—no, you won't take my money, I know—but there'd be no better use for some of Mum's money than helping you achieve your dream.'

Meg stared at him, unable to take in the enormity of what had just occurred between them.

'Here's your hat, what's your hurry? That's what you're saying, Sam?' The words crept out past strangled vocal cords.

He didn't answer, just stared out to sea.

She waited, counted waves, counted some more, then picked up a handful of chips and flung them at him, rising to her feet at the same time and racing from the beach.

Across the park, up the hill, panting for breath, running from pain, hating Sam so much she wanted to yell her rage to the sky.

He let her go, the damage done, his own pain suggesting he'd found out exactly what she talked about when she talked of deep-down love.

Benjie came back in for his treatment, and Meg was by his bed, talking to Jenny about Ben's progress, when the alarm sounded.

The number flashing in the light-box above the

door told her it was the nursery, and she knew it would be Melody's baby.

'There's no apparent reason for it,' Mike Chan was saying to Sam as Meg flew through the door.

She looked around. No crash cart?

'You're not resuscitating?'

She heard the accusation in her voice but couldn't stop it.

'We tried, Meg,' Sam said gently. 'Fingertip heart massage, oxygen—'

'That's all? No drugs? No defibrillation?'

'She's less than a week old, Meg. Shocking her isn't an option. It's too extreme for a neonate.' He glanced up at the clock on the wall. 'Time of death, ten twenty-one a.m.

'You can't do that! Just decide like that. We should try again—try drugs. We can't just give in!' Bright spots of colour now in Meg's cheeks, and anguish in her eyes.

Instinct took Sam towards her. He grasped her arm with a firm hand and said, as gently as he could, 'We can't save her, Meg.'

The hectic colour faded, leaving her ashen

grey, her body shaking as if she was about to collapse. He tightened his hold on her, fearing she'd faint—trying to get her away from the cot, away from the other staff.

But just as quickly as it had ebbed, her strength returned. She straightened, disengaging herself from his hold and walking away.

Acting as if nothing had happened—although her shaking hands gave lie to the pretence.

He caught up with her in the alcove and led her outside into the tropical gardens, to a seat beneath an old fig tree, its drooping branches hiding them from prying eyes.

'I should be talking to Melody and Mrs Carter,' she said, her voice muffled by tears. 'Not falling apart like this.'

'Mike Chan will talk to them and we'll see them later.'

She didn't answer, weeping quietly against his chest while his arms held her close and his head made silent promises he couldn't—shouldn't—keep.

At last she straightened, the pale skin blotched and streaked with tears. He took out his handkerchief and wiped it for her, then held her close again, rocking her in his arms.

'I don't think I cried for Lucy,' she whispered. 'Not properly. I was down in Melbourne on my own. I had to do things, sign things, organise a funeral, so I kept pretending everything was all right and pretending became a habit.'

She looked up and tried a feeble smile.

'So I guess I didn't grieve properly either and it was all bottled up inside me just waiting to come flooding out.'

She found her own handkerchief and blew her nose.

'On you. I'm sorry. I know it's not what you want.'

Sam heard the curses building like bubbling lava inside him, and barely kept them to a muted roar when they came out.

'Don't ever say that,' he finally managed. 'You and every part of you is what I want. Do you really think I only want the happy bits—the sex, the fun, the companionship? Do you think I don't want to share your pain? To hold you when you cry? Do you really think I'm so shallow, Megan, that holding you like this would bother me?'

He took her face in his hands and turned it towards him.

'You gave me one great gift a few days ago when you told me Lucy's name. Letting me hold you while you cried was another gift, Meg. I love you. You must know that! You must know in *your* bones that my love is just as deep as yours!'

'But…'

He gathered her close again, and held her to him, knowing exactly what she'd been unable to say.

And suddenly *he* knew, too. He'd been wrong, taking a unilateral decision not to tell her about the heart disease, instead making out she was asking too much of love.

'I thought it best,' he began. 'Best if we just broke up. That way you'd get over me, finish medicine, find someone else to love and have your babies.'

She shifted in his arms, pushing away from his body so she could see his face.

So he could see her disbelief…

'Best for whom?'

'For you.'

'Breaking my heart was best for me? Because you didn't love me enough, you decided it should end?'

Would she understand?

'Because I *did* love you enough,' he said. 'Because I finally understood the kind of love you wanted—*felt* that kind of love for you. I thought it was the kind of love that should put the loved one first—before everything. But finding it—understanding it—came about because of something else I learned.'

He kissed her lips, cold and still damp from her tears, then straightened up and took her hands in his.

'I spoke to Martin Goodall. Mum was seeing him for a heart problem all her working life. If she had a faulty valve way back then, I can only assume it was congenital. You wanted babies, Meg. You'd already had one baby with a heart problem. Could I father babies with you without risk of that happening again?'

She was frowning furiously at him, as if unable to believe what she was hearing.

'You pushed me away, decided we weren't meant to be together, in the name of love, for heaven's sake—because you were worried our babies might have heart problems?'

He nodded.

'Without telling me? Without talking about it? Without genetic testing? For all you know, your mother's problem might have come from rheumatic fever when she was a child—nothing to do with genetics. And isn't that what you did thirteen years ago? Pushed me away without an explanation, a discussion—anything? This is exactly what happened then. The decision was all yours! Taking control and throwing me out of your life as if I was nothing more than an old pair of jeans.'

Rheumatic fever? Why hadn't he thought of that?

He was so busy feeling relief he missed what Meg was saying next, but from the look on her face it wasn't something he particularly wanted to hear. She was still furious.

She stood up and glared down at him.

'I think it's a very good thing you decided, for whatever pathetic reason, we weren't suited to each other, because two more stupid people I've never met. Babies! We'd be lucky to breed chimpanzees, and stupid chimpanzees at that!'

She marched away, not back into the hospital but towards the car park, escaping him as well as her memories.

She'd walk along the beach, he guessed. Maybe she'd cool off enough to talk some more.

Not likely!

He went back into the hospital to talk to Melody about the baby she hadn't wanted.

She was sitting up in bed, alone in the single room, tears dribbling down her cheeks. Having passed Mrs Carter and Mike in the corridor, Sam knew she knew and he took her hand and sat beside her, letting her fingers cling to his.

'I kept saying I didn't want her and now she's dead,' Melody cried, lifting her other hand to her mouth and biting at her knuckles.

'Not because of anything you said,' Sam reminded her.

'But because of what I did. Of how I was.'

Her anguish was so great Sam stood up and put his arm around her, holding her against his chest as he'd held Meg earlier.

Holding another young woman while she cried for another baby.

Then suddenly she straightened, grabbed a tissue and mopped her face.

'That's it, Dr Agostini. Oh, I know I've been going along with the drug protocol you've set for me, but in my heart of hearts I haven't believed it would work—haven't really cared if it did or didn't. But say I had another baby—did this to it. No way!'

Her lips wobbled as if this new resolve wasn't quite as strong as it should be.

'It won't be easy,' Sam reminded her, 'but there are excellent places you can go for help.'

Melody nodded, and even found a smile. 'Mum knows every one of them, but this time it will be different. This time I'll be doing it for me—and for the baby—not for Mum or to escape a jail sentence, or any other reason.'

'That's a great start,' Sam agreed, 'and if you need more incentive, by the time you're clean I should be about ready to open a rehab centre up here. Would you like to come back and work there?'

Melody smiled her thanks then reached for the tissues again as all the brave talk of the future didn't completely blot out the loss of her baby.

'Don't be afraid to cry,' Sam told her. 'Crying's part of the healing process.'

She gave him a watery smile, and as Mrs Carter came back into the room, Sam had the strong impression that Melody might just make it.

He went back to his office, finished up some paperwork, then drove to the site of the new hospital. The architect was there, discussing final landscaping details with a contractor. With the painting nearly done, the place was looking great.

'You'll be opening right on time,' he told Sam, leading him into the foyer to show him the new glass walls that had been put in place behind the reception desk. 'When's your manager due to start?'

Thoughts of Megan had pushed the details of the hospital completion out of Sam's head, but he recalled his manager, who'd been in Sydney handling the ordering of all the necessary equipment, was due to arrive in the Bay this

coming weekend and start work here the following Monday.

'Great,' the architect replied. 'We'll have his
office all set up by then, and he can handle any
queries we might have over the last few weeks.'

Sam accompanied the man around the building,
approving of all that had happened since his
previous visit two days earlier, then, leaving the
man with a plumber in the staff washrooms, he
walked back out the front to admire the healthy
coconut palms that had been planted just that day.

'It's beautiful.'

Meg!

The words were still husky from her tears, but
her face showed no sign of the emotional
storm—storms—she'd suffered, although her
cheeks held the pinkness of embarrassment as
she forced herself to look him in the eyes.

'Want to see inside?' he offered, unsure exactly
what was happening here but inwardly excited
just to be near Meg again.

She nodded and he led her in, taking her away
from where the architect and plumber were,
showing her the day surgery rooms, then the

main theatre, explaining how the design allowed for the necessary clean zones to prevent contamination.

'Have you got a store cupboard?' she asked, her voice shaking so much it was a wonder she got them out.

Sam had to smile, and he put his arm around her shoulders and led her into the scrub room. Closed the door and leaned against it.

'Not a store cupboard but not much bigger. Will it do?'

Meg nodded her reply then studied him in silence, eventually shrugging her shoulders as she stumbled into speech.

'I don't know where we are, Sam. I don't know if we even have a relationship any more. I'm lost. But I do know that I love you and that comes first. Before plans, or babies, or anything else. I don't even know if you want to hear that, but I had to say it.'

Green eyes pleaded with him, but for what? Every instinct in his body told him to be careful—that this was potentially the most important moment in his life.

But Meg was lost and scared, so what could he do but take her in his arms and hold her close, pressing kisses on her hair as he fought for breath to say the words he had to say?

'You didn't know if I wanted to hear it? Of course I wanted to hear it, Megan. I love you so much, bone-deep, Meg. I know that now. But before I'd even told you how much, I did my best to ruin everything for both of us.'

He tipped her head back and kissed her properly on the lips.

'But it's still an issue, Mum's heart problem, and we have to talk about genetic testing and all the practical things, but now I understand exactly what you meant—that love is about sharing as well as about loving. And sharing is about bad times—bad things—as well as good.'

He kissed her again and felt her mouth grow warm and her tongue tease along his lips.

'I love you that way, Megan, and every other way. I love your compassion and your humour and the way you walk across the sand, shaking the sand off your toes the way the cat does. I even love your splashy swimming, and especially I love your sexy underwear, most of which is still living in my house.'

Another kiss, much longer this time, then he lifted his head to ask, 'Come and live with it? Live properly with me? Marry me whenever, but shift out of the cottage and share my house as well as my life? Now?'

Meg kissed him this time, pressing her lips to his, while her heart sang with a new happiness—bone-deep!

CHAPTER ELEVEN

THE BEACH at sunset, Meg in a filmy golden skirt that blew against her legs and a lacy, beaded top that dipped between her breasts, the golden colour making her skin seem whiter. Two gardenias pinned in her hair, feet bare but for the sand that clung to them.

Mrs Anstey, Bill, the Richards family, his manager and Meg's friends from the hospital. Eddie stood beside him, Meg's cousin Libby beside her, Meg shaking as much as he'd been shaking—excited yet somehow terrified that something might still go wrong. Excited yet somehow terrified by the magnitude of his love...

Sam rolled over so he could tuck his body around his wife's, spooning into her back so he could feel the warmth and softness of her against his skin.

She moved, snuggling closer, then turned and put her arms around his neck.

'Did we really do it?' she whispered, moving her head to his pillow so her lips were only inches from his own.

'Get married?' Sam lifted his left hand from beneath the sheet and held it so she would see it.

'I guess we did.'

Then he found her hand and brought it out as well, so their two hands intertwined, the new gold rings glinting in the moonlight that streamed through the windows of the old house.

'Did I mention love, Mrs Agostini?'